THE PHANTOM
OF THE OPERA

AN ADAPTED CLASSIC

THE PHANTOM OF THE OPERA

GASTON LEROUX

GLOBE BOOK COMPANY
A Division of Simon & Schuster
Englewood Cliffs, New Jersey

Adaptation: Mary Ansaldo

Cover Design: Mike McIver Graphics

Cover Illustration and Interior Illustrations: Gershon Griffith

ISBN: 835-90476-8

Printed in the United States of America

5 6 7 8 9 10

GLOBE BOOK COMPANY
A Division of Simon & Schuster
Englewood Cliffs, New Jersey

CONTENTS

ABOUT THE AUTHOR

The French author Gaston Leroux was best known during his lifetime as a writer of detective fiction. His amateur detective character, Joseph Rouletabille, is a young crime reporter who uses his reasoning powers to solve mysteries while the police are still looking for clues. Leroux was a big, red-bearded man, known in France at the turn of the century as a great reporter. He would go anywhere and risk his life for a good story. He began to write novels in his late thirties. All his novels were originally written as serials for Parisian magazines or daily newspapers. Leroux's greatest success was *The Mystery of the Yellow Room* (1907), called by the English writer Arnold Bennett "the most dazzlingly brilliant detective story I have ever read." Outside of detective fiction, Leroux was best known as a writer of horror fiction. In addition to *Phantom*, he wrote *The Double Life of Theophraste Longuet* and *The Queen of the Sabbath*.

ADAPTER'S NOTE

In preparing this edition of *The Phantom of the Opera*, we have kept closely to what Gaston Leroux wrote. We have modified some of Leroux's vocabulary and shortened and simplified many of his sentences and paragraphs. None of the story, however, has been omitted. Certain French words, titles, and expressions have been retained to give the book a French flavor. They have all been translated and explained in footnotes.

INTRODUCTION

In *The Phantom of the Opera*, Gaston Leroux wrote a story with several layers. In all of the layers, we find humor and suspense. But first of all, *The Phantom of the Opera* is a love story.

It is the story of a love between the young singer Christine Daaé and a mysterious presence she calls the Angel of Music. It is also the story of the love of Christine and Raoul, a young nobleman. Leroux's characters experience the happiness and despair, disappointment and triumph, deceit and self-sacrifice that make up a love story.

Secondly, *The Phantom of the Opera* is a mystery, a ghost story. Is there really a ghost who frequents the Opera? Who is this monster who lives in the cellars? And what is the elusive Persian's role in all this?

Finally, *The Phantom of the Opera* is rich in factual detail. Its setting is the Paris Opera House—the largest and most complex theater in the world. Gaston Leroux used the Paris Opera House as it really is. It is not a building created from his imagination. To understand much of the story, one should try to visualize this magnificent building—its grand spaces, its vast underground cellars, and its miles of passageways.

The Paris Opera House

The Paris Opera House, begun in 1861 during France's Second Empire and finished in 1875 during the Third Republic, is the most complete building of its kind in the world, and in many respects the most beautiful. No other city possesses an opera house so comprehensive in plan and execution, and none can boast a building so splendid.

Paris was the world center of the performing arts

during the 19th century, particularly of opera, and it remained so until well into the twentieth century. Composers of every country dreamed of having their operas performed there.

In 1860 a competition was held by the French government for the design of a new Paris Opera House. The winning design was submitted by a largely unknown 35-year-old architect named Charles Garnier. The challenge was a great one.

Since the French public loved spectacle and elaborate stagings, the new opera house had to incorporate the best, most advanced stage equipment and technology. At the same time, the French government wanted the public spaces of the new opera house to be as beautiful as those of a great royal palace. The opera goer should be surrounded with art and luxury and feel privileged to be at a performance.

Charles Garnier gave the French government everything it wanted—at great expense—and he did so brilliantly. Until the end of World War I, when architectural styles began to change, Garnier's opera house was the most admired modern building in the world. In France, the building is referred to as the Palais Garnier—the Garnier Palace.

The construction site for the Paris Opera House was chosen in 1861. The various uses of the building—ballet and opera—required a very strong and deep foundation. For example, sets up to fifty feet high would be raised and lowered on the stage. It was necessary to lay a foundation that could support a weight of 22,000,000 pounds.

The builders soon discovered a large underground lake at the site. While the excavation went on, eight pumps worked around the clock for seven months to keep out the water. After the excavation was done and the massive foundation and extensive cellars were completed, a large lake was left in the deepest cellar. This lake is the locale of some of the more sinister scenes in *The Phantom of the Opera*.

The stage area of the Paris Opera is larger than the auditorium. The actual stage is deep enough to hold such scenes as shipwrecks at sea and frozen rivers with ice skaters gliding about. The machinery to create these stage wonders is all there. In addition to the performing area with its soaring ceiling (the flies) and wings, there are 80 private dressing rooms for the artists, each with an antechamber, dressing area, and closet. There are other areas to accomodate 538 people dressing and preparing for a performance.

When the Paris Opera opened, there were seventy carpenters on staff for the building of scenery, with proportionate numbers of stagehands, make-up artists, costumers, lighting experts (gas men in the 19th century), and all the other people who made performances happen.

All of this was *behind* the scenes. Out front, the auditorium was lavishly decorated in gilded plaster, carved wood, and velvet. Even today, when there is a well-dressed audience in attendance, there is almost as much to see in the auditorium as there is on stage.

Beyond that are the many art-filled public rooms and rehearsal rooms. Perhaps the most spectacular sight is the Grand Stairway, which rises from street level near the entrance to the house to the central landing. It is constructed of different colored marbles and rises majestically to the main landing. Climbing or descending this stairway gives the visitor the feeling of actually participating in some magnificent performance. To the right and left of the landing are stairs to the level of the first row of boxes. It is on this level that Box 5, which figures prominently in *The Phantom of the Opera*, is found.

Gaston Leroux knew that he could count on his readers' fascination with this great building. Since its opening in 1875, it has been a center of national interest—and intense gossip. Every production, every artistic decision at the Opera is national news in France, and everyone has an opinion, whether they like opera or not.

Leroux's *The Phantom of the Opera*, published in 1910, was not his most successful work. (That distinction went to his *Mystery of the Yellow Room*.) The fame of *The Phantom of the Opera* is mainly due to Hollywood. The landmark film of 1925, featuring the brilliant performance of Lon Chaney, placed Leroux's novel among such celebrated works as *Frankenstein* and *Dracula*.

There have been at least five subsequent film versions of *The Phantom of the Opera*, but none of them is really faithful to the novel. Characters are added or dropped, and the story is always changed. One version takes place in London, another in Budapest! So far, no film has used the actual Paris Opera House as a location for the important scenes.

The Phantom of the Opera has been revived most recently by the English composer Andrew Lloyd Webber as one of the most popular musical stage shows ever produced.

To understand why people continue to return to Leroux's haunting story, one must read the novel. No film has captured the strange relationships between the main characters or the eerie atmosphere of fear that pervades the great theater.

Characters

Mlle. Christine Daaé	*A young soprano at the Opera*
Viscount Raoul de Chagny	*A young nobleman, in love with Christine Daaé*
Count Philippe de Chagny	*His older brother and guardian*
M. Faure	*Police magistrate*
The Persian	*Friend of the Opera Ghost*
MM. Debienne and Poligny	*Outgoing managers of the Opera*
La Sorelli	*Leading ballerina of the Opera*
Mlle. Jammes	*Ballerina at the Opera*
Mlle. "Meg" Giry	*Ballerina at the Opera*
Mme. Giry	*Her mother, an usherette*
M. Joseph Buquet	*Chief scene-changer at the Opera*
MM. Armand Moncharmin and Firmin Richard	*New managers of the Opera*
M. Gabriel	*Chorus master at the Opera*
M. Mercier	*Acting coach of the Opera*
M. Rémy	*Secretary at the Opera*
M. Lachenel	*Head groom of the Opera*
M. Valérius	*Christine Daaé's music teacher and adoptive father*
Mme. Valérius	*His wife*
Carlotta	*Leading soprano of the Opera*
M. Mifroid	*Paris police commissioner*
M. Mauclair	*Gas man of the Opera*

Prologue

How the Author Learned that the
Opera Ghost Really Existed

The Opera ghost was real. He was not, as many thought, a figment of the imagination of all who worked at the Opera. He was a real person, but he did assume the form of a phantom, a ghost.

When I went through the archives of the National Academy of Music, I was struck by some remarkable coincidences. There had been a series of mysterious events surrounding the kidnapping of singer Christine Daaé, the disappearance of Viscount Chagny, and the death of his older brother Count Philippe. No one had connected these tragedies with the actions of the supposed ghost. But I came to see the truth.

One day, leaving the library after hours of useless labor, I ran into a friend. He was chatting with a lively, well-groomed elderly man and eagerly introduced us. I had been trying to find the examining magistrate in the Chagny case, a man named Faure. The older man was Monsieur Faure himself, just returned from fifteen years in Canada.

Faure had heard the stories of an abnormal being that lived in the Opera house, and he knew the story of the envelope. He had listened to the testimony of the man called "the Persian," who claimed to have met the ghost often. But he remained convinced that the Viscount was insane and that the Count had died accidentally. The Persian, he thought, was just a mystic.

With my first bit of good luck I found the Persian in his apartment in Paris. He told me he knew all about the ghost, and he gave me his proof, including the strange letters of Christine Daaé. I verified the handwriting as hers, and I checked the background of the Persian. If I had had doubts before, I was now convinced. The ghost was not a myth! My belief was bolstered by friends of the Chagny family who saw my documents. One of them wrote to me, saying

> . . . if it be possible to explain the tragedy through the ghost, then I beg you, sir, to talk to us about the ghost again. Mysterious though the ghost may at first appear, he will always be more easily explained than the dismal story in which malevolent people have tried to picture two brothers killing each other who had worshipped each other all their lives.

Finally I went back to the Opera house. An important discovery confirmed what the Persian had told me. You will remember that, when workmen were digging up the cellars of the Opera before burying the records of the artist's voice, they had found a corpse. The newspapers claimed it was a victim of the Commune.[1] I could prove that this was not the case. In my research I had discovered that these poor people, massacred in the cellars of the Opera, had been buried on the other side of the cellars.

But we will return to the matter of the corpse later. For now, I want to thank Monsieur Mifroid (the

---

1. **Commune**   During the Revolution of 1871, the Opera House building fell into the hands of the Commune, an early communist group, which ruled for a few months. During that time, many aristocrats were captured and killed. Some bodies were buried under the Opera House.

commissioner of police called in after Christine Daaé disappeared), Monsieur Rémy, (former managers' secretary), Monsieur Gabriel (former chorus-master), and particularly the Baroness de Castelot-Barbezac (the "little Meg" of the story, and oldest daughter of the woman who had charge of the ghost's private box). These people were all of great help to me. Thanks to them, I am able to portray for you—in their smallest details—this story of sheer love and terror.

I also want to thank the present management of the Opera and Monsieur Gabion, the architect responsible for preserving the building. And lastly, my friend Monsieur J. Le Croze who gave me access to his theatrical library.

GASTON LEROUX

1 *Is It the Ghost?*

The story begins on the night the managers of the Opera—Messieurs[1] Debienne and Poligny—were giving a gala performance to mark their retirement. La Sorelli, one of the principal dancers of the company, was alone in her dressing room running through the speech she was to give for the retiring managers. Suddenly her room was invaded by a half dozen young dancers, some laughing hysterically, some crying with terror. It was little Jammes—of the tip-tilted nose, the forget-me-not eyes, the rose-red cheeks, and lily-white neck and shoulders—who gave the explanation in a trembling voice:

"It's the ghost!" And she locked the door.

Sorelli shuddered at the mention of the ghost and called little Jammes a "silly little fool." Then, as she believed in ghosts in general, and in the Opera ghost in particular, she quickly asked for details:

"Have you seen him?"

"As plainly as I see you now," moaned little Jammes, dropping into a chair.

Little Giry—the one with black eyes, hair black as ink, dark complexion, and little bones—added, "If that's the ghost, he's very ugly."

"Oh, yes!" cried the girls from the *corps de ballet*.[2]

---

1. **Messieurs** plural form of the French title *Monsieur*, which means "Mister," used with two or more men before their names or titles
2. ***corps de ballet*** troupe of ballet dancers—those who do not perform solo

They all began to talk at once. The ghost had appeared to them as a gentleman dressed in evening clothes. He had suddenly stood before them in the passageway. They didn't know where he had come from. He seemed to have come right through the wall.

"Nonsense!" said one of the dancers, who had more or less kept her head. "You see the ghost everywhere!"

That was true. For months, the only thing discussed at the Opera had been this ghost dressed in evening clothes who roamed the building top to bottom like a shadow. He spoke to nobody; nobody dared speak to him. He vanished as soon as he was seen; nobody knew how or where. Of course, being a ghost, he made no noise when he walked. People began by laughing and making fun of this spook in undertaker's clothes. But soon the legend swelled to enormous proportion among the *corps de ballet*. All the girls claimed to have seen him, and those who laughed the loudest were the most ill at ease. Even when he remained unseen, there were accidents, both comic and serious, for which he was held responsible. If someone fell or lost something, it was the ghost at work.

The Opera ghost was no ordinary man in evening dress. The evening suit covered a skeleton. At least, so the ballet girls said. And, of course, it had a death's head.

Actually the idea of the skeleton and death's head had come from Joseph Buquet, the chief scene-changer for the Opera. Buquet had really seen the ghost and had given this description:

"He is extraordinarily thin and his suit hangs on a skeleton frame. His eyes are so deep you can hardly see his pupils. You just see two dark holes, as in a dead man's skull. His skin is stretched across his bones, and it is a nasty yellow color. His nose is so little you can't see it from the side, and the absence of the nose is horrible to look at. The only hair he has is three or four long, dark locks on his forehead and behind his ears."

Now since the scene changer was a serious man not given to imagining things, this description was received with interest and amazement. Soon others began to say that they too had seen the man dressed in evening clothes with a death's head on his shoulders. Some said that Joseph Buquet was the victim of a practical joke played by one of his assistants. But then, one after another, there came a series of accidents so strange and unexplainable that even the most skeptical people began to feel nervous.

A fireman had gone to inspect the cellars and ventured a little farther than usual. Suddenly he appeared on the stage, pale, shaking, and near to collapse. He had, he reported, seen something coming towards him at eye level—*a head of fire with no body attached to it!* This story gave the dancers— leaders, front-row dancers and back-row alike— plenty of excuse to be nervous in dark corners and badly lighted passageways. If a fireman could faint from fright, why should they not be fearful as well? While the fireman's story did not exactly match Buquet's, the young ladies persuaded themselves that the ghost had several heads, which he changed as he pleased. Sorelli herself, after hearing the fireman's story, placed a horseshoe on a table near the stage door. Everyone was to touch it before setting foot on the stairs.

But back to the evening in question.

"It's the ghost?" little Jammes had cried.

A terrible silence now reigned in Sorelli's dressing room. At last, little Jammes whispered:

"Listen!"

There was a rustling sound outside the door. No one heard footsteps: just a sound like silk sliding over the panel. Then it stopped.

Sorelli, trying to show more bravery than the girls, went to the door and said in a shaky voice:

"Is there anyone there?"

Little Meg Giry held Sorelli back by her skirt. "Whatever you do, don't open the door!"

But Sorelli, armed with the dagger that she always carried, turned the key and pulled open the door. The ballet girls retreated into the back of the dressing room.

There was no one there.

"Still we saw him!" little Jammes declared. "He must be prowling around somewhere. We had better go down together, at once, for 'the speech.' And we will all come back up together."

She touched the coral ring she wore as a good luck piece. Sorelli secretly used her thumbnail to make the cross of Saint Andrew on the wooden ring she wore, but she said to the young women:

"Come, children, pull yourselves together. I'm certain no one has ever really seen the ghost!"

"Yes, yes, we saw him!" cried the girls. "With his death's head and his evening clothes."

"And Gabriel saw him, too," added Jammes. "Only yesterday . . . in broad daylight."

"Gabriel, the chorus master?"

"Yes, didn't you know?"

"And he was wearing his evening clothes in broad daylight?"

"Who? Gabriel?"

"No, the ghost!"

"Certainly. That's how he knew him. Gabriel had been in the stage manager's office when suddenly the Persian came in. You know that the Persian has the evil eye. . . ."

"Oh, yes!" cried the ballet girls, each warding off evil by making the common sign. This gesture involved pointing their first and little fingers at the absent Persian, with their middle two fingers curved in toward the palm and held by the thumb.

"And you know how superstitious Gabriel is!" continued Jammes. "But he is polite when he meets the Persian. He just puts his hand in his pocket and touches his keys so as to touch iron. Well, anyway, he saw the Persian in the doorway and he jumped up to touch the iron lock on the cupboard. In doing that, he tore his coat on a nail. In his haste to get out of the room, he banged his head on a coat peg. Then stepping back he skinned his arm on a screen near the piano. He tried to catch his balance on the piano but the lid fell on his fingers and crushed them. He rushed out of the office like a madman, slipped on the stairs and fell on his back down the whole flight. I was just passing by with Mother. We picked him up. He was covered with bruises and his face was all bloody. We were frightened out of our lives, but *he* thanked the Lord for having escaped so easily. Then he told us what had frightened him. Behind the Persian he had seen *the ghost with the death's head*, just as in Joseph Buquet's description!"

After her story, there was a silence. It was broken by Giry.

"Joseph Buquet should keep quiet."

"Why should he?" asked someone.

"That's what Mother thinks," replied Meg.

"And why does your mother think that?"

"Because . . . because . . . nothing," Meg stammered.

The young women crowded around her. They stood side by side, leaning forward, communicating their terror to one another.

"I swore not to tell!" gasped Meg.

The young ladies gave her no peace and promised to keep the secret if she told it. Finally she began:

"It's because of the private box. The ghost's box! It's Box 5. You know, next to the stage box, on the left. That's the ghost's box. No one has had it for over a month, except the ghost. And orders have been given at the box office that it must never be sold."

"And does the ghost really come there?"

"Yes."

"Then someone must have seen him in there!"

"That's just it! The ghost is not seen. He has no evening clothes! And all that talk about a death's head or a head on fire is nonsense! There's nothing to that. You only *hear* him when he is in the box. Mother has never seen him, but she has heard him. Mother knows, because she gives him his program. But . . . I should have held my tongue. If Mother finds out I've told you. . . . But Joseph Buquet had no business saying those things about the ghost. It will bring him bad luck. Mother said so last night."

There was a sound of heavy feet in the passage and a breathless voice cried:

"Cécile! Cécile! Are you there?"

Jammes opened the door and her mother—a large woman—burst into the room and dropped groaning into a vacant armchair. Her eyes rolled madly.

"Joseph Buquet is dead!" she moaned.

The room exploded with exclamations, outcries, and requests for explanations.

"He was found hanging in the third-floor cellar."

"It's the ghost!" little Giry blurted out. But right away she covered her mouth: "I didn't say that. I didn't say that!"

Sorelli was very pale. "I will never be able to give my speech," she muttered.

The truth is that no one ever found out how Joseph Buquet died. Monsieur Moncharmin, one of the new managers of the Opera, wrote a description of what happened when Mercier, the acting-manager, came darting into his office:

> . . . He seemed half mad and told me that the body of a scene-changer had been found hanging in the third cellar under the stage. I shouted:
>
> "Come and cut him down!"
>
> By the time I had rushed down the staircase and the Jacob's ladder,[3] the man was no longer hanging from his rope!

The coroner called it "natural suicide," but it seems very *unnatural* to me. First a man is found hanging from a rope and then, when they go to cut him down, the rope has disappeared. M.[4] Moncharmin suggested that the dancing girls might have taken the rope as a precaution against the evil eye. But can you imagine the *corps de ballet* charging down the Jacob's ladder and dividing up the suicide's rope before anyone else arrived? When I think of where the body was discovered—in the third cellar underneath the stage—I am sure *somebody* made certain that the rope disappeared after it had

---

3. **Jacob's ladder** rope ladder, with wooden steps
4. **M.** abbreviation for the French title Monsieur, meaning "Mister" or "sir"

served its purpose. Time will show if I am wrong.

The news spread quickly. The dressing rooms emptied, and the ballet girls, huddled around Sorelli like sheep around their shepherdess, headed for the foyer[5] as fast as their little pink legs could carry them.

---

5. foyer kind of hall/reception/practice area

2 *The New Marguerite*

On the first landing, Sorelli ran into the Comte[1] de Chagny, who was coming upstairs. Generally a calm person, the count seemed very excited.

"I was just coming to see you," he said. "What an evening! And what a triumph Christine Daaé was!"

"Impossible!" said Meg Giry. "Six months ago she couldn't sing a note! But let us by," continued the girl sassily. "We are on our way to see about a man who was found hanging by his neck."

Just then the acting-manager passed by. "Please don't let Messieurs Debienne and Poligny hear about it," he exclaimed. "It would upset them on their last day."

And they all went on to the foyer, which was filled with people talking about the performance. The Comte de Chagny was right: it had been a triumph. All the great composers of the day had conducted their works. And Christine Daaé had revealed a voice that astonished the audience. She had begun by singing some passages from *Roméo et Juliette*,[2] in a voice that listeners called angelic. But that was nothing compared to superhuman notes she had sung in the prison scene and final trio from *Faust*.[3] She had performed in place

---

1. **Comte** French word for *Count* (In this story, both the French and English titles are used.)
2. ***Roméo et Juliette*** French opera by Charles Gounod, based on Shakespeare's play of the same name
3. ***Faust*** French opera by Charles Gounod, based on the German poet Goethe's play of the same name

of La Carlotta, who was ill. No one had ever heard anything like it.

Daaé had created a splendid new Marguerite, the heroine in *Faust*. The audience went wild, rising to its feet and shouting, cheering, clapping. Christine sobbed and fainted, and had to be carried off stage. Some of the audience were puzzled. Why had this great talent been kept from them all this time? Daaé had sung well before, but never like this! Why had Christine been asked to stand in for Carlotta? Did the managers know of her hidden talent? If so, why had they kept it hidden? Why had the singer herself kept it hidden? The whole thing was a mystery.

The Comte de Chagny, standing in his box, also applauded loudly. Philippe Georges Marie, Comte de Chagny was forty-one years old and a great aristocrat. He was a good-looking man, taller than average with good features in spite of a hard forehead and cold eyes. He was very polite to women and a little snobbish to men, which did not gain him favor. He had a good heart and conscience. His father, the old Count Philibert, had died leaving a great deal of property. His two sisters and young brother, Raoul, had refused to divide the estate. Instead, they had left it all in Philippe's hands as the oldest. When his two sisters married, Philippe gave each of them her share as a wedding gift.

Philippe's mother had died giving birth to Raoul. At the time of his father's death, Philippe was thirty-two and Raoul, just twelve. Philippe quickly took over the upbringing of his little brother. He was assisted for a time by an elderly aunt who lived in Brest. It was there that Raoul acquired a taste for the sea. He entered a program on a training ship and made a trip around the world. He had just been appointed as a member of an Arctic Circle expedition and was enjoying a six-month leave before departing.

Raoul was very shy—almost innocent. Indulged by his two sisters and elderly aunt, Raoul had a charming way about him. At twenty-one, he looked eighteen. He had a small moustache, blue eyes and the complexion of a girl.

Philippe also spoiled Raoul. He was proud of his naval career and eagerly showed him all the sights in Paris. He took Raoul along wherever he went, including the foyer of the ballet. Philippe was said to be very friendly with Sorelli, and he often spent time with her after dinner. He had plenty of leisure time, and Sorelli had the finest eyes he had ever seen! Furthermore, the foyer of the ballet at the Opera was one of the places to be seen in Paris society!

Philippe might not have taken his young brother backstage, but Raoul had repeatedly asked him to. On the night in question, amidst the wild applause, Philippe looked at Raoul and noticed that he was very pale.

"Don't you see the woman is fainting? Let's go and see," Raoul said. "She never sang like this before."

Philippe seemed pleased at his brother's interest, and they soon made their way to the door. Raoul was very impatient as they fought the crowds going in the same direction. In his impatience, he tore his gloves without realizing it. Philippe was too kind to laugh at his brother, but now he understood why Raoul had lately seemed absent-minded and always wanted to talk about the Opera.

Raoul led the way through the crowd of gentlemen, scene-changers, supers, and chorus girls. His face was set with passion, making Philippe smile as he hurried to follow the young man. They made their way through the rush of ballet girls and into a passageway where the cries "Daaé! Daaé!" still echoed. The count was surprised that Raoul knew the way, since he had never taken him to the dressing rooms before. Postponing his nightly visit to Sorelli, he followed Raoul down the passage toward Daaé's room, where they met a crowd that had gathered in amazement over Christine's success as well as her fainting spell. Christine still had not come to, and the doctor had just arrived. Thus it was that she awakened lying in the arms of Raoul, being tended by the doctor. At the young man's suggestion, the doctor cleared the room. Christine came to slowly in the company of only her maid, the doctor, and Raoul—whom the two others assumed had some right to be present.

Philippe, pushed outside in the passageway with all the others, was amused. "Oh, that devil! He *is* a Chagny after all!" Laughing, he turned and made his way toward Sorelli's dressing room. He met her on the way, surrounded by her group of trembling girls, as we have seen.

Meanwhile, Christine Daaé saw Raoul and gave a start. She looked at him, then looked with a smile at the doctor, then at her maid, then again at Raoul.

"Monsieur," she whispered, "who are you?"

"Mademoiselle,"[4] replied Raoul, kissing her hand, *"I am the little boy who went into the sea to rescue your scarf."*

Christine looked again at the doctor and maid, and all three laughed.

Raoul, very red, replied, "Mademoiselle, since you refuse to recognize me, I would like to speak to you alone; it's very important."

"When I am better, do you mind? You have been

---

4. **Mademoiselle** French title for unmarried woman or girl

very kind," she said, her voice shaking. The doctor agreed.

Suddenly Christine stood up and announced with unexpected energy, "I am not ill now. Thank you, Doctor. I would like to be alone. Please, all of you go away. Leave me alone. I feel very restless this evening."

The doctor left and Raoul found himself alone in the passageway. This part of the theater was deserted now, since the farewell ceremony was taking place in the foyer. He hid himself in the shadow of a doorway, hoping Christine would emerge to attend the event. He still felt a terrible pain in his heart, and it was this that he wanted to talk to her about right away.

Suddenly, the door opened and the maid came out, carrying some bundles. When he asked her about the condition of her mistress, she replied laughing that she was well but wanted to be left alone. It occurred to Raoul that perhaps Christine wanted to be left alone for *him*. Had he not said he wanted to speak to her alone?

Hardly breathing, Raoul approached the door and started to knock. But his hand dropped when he heard a man's voice saying in a masterful tone:

"Christine, you must love me!"

And Christine's voice, sad and trembling as if she were crying, replied:

"How can you talk like that? *When I sing only for you!*"

Raoul's heart throbbed loudly. The whole passageway seemed to echo with its deafening sound. If the sound continued, they would hear it inside the room. They would open the door and he would be disgraced. What a thing for a Chagny! To be caught listening at a door! He held his chest with both hands to make it stop.

The man spoke again:

"Are you very tired?"

"Oh, tonight I gave you my soul and I am dead!" Christine replied.

"Your soul is a beautiful thing, child," said the man's voice, "and I thank you. No emperor ever received so fair a gift. *The angels wept tonight.*"

Raoul heard nothing after that, but he did not leave. He returned to the dark corner, determined to wait until the man left. At one and the same time, he had learned what love and hatred meant. He knew whom he loved. He wanted to see whom he hated. To his astonishment, the door opened and Christine Daaé appeared, wrapped in furs and with her face hidden by a veil. She was alone. She closed the door but did not lock it. She passed Raoul. He did not even follow her with his eyes, for they were fixed on the door, which did not open again.

He crossed the passageway to the door, opened it, went in, and shut the door. He was in absolute darkness. The light had been turned out.

"I know you're here," said Raoul, with his back against the door. "Why are you hiding?"

There was only darkness and silence. Raoul heard only the sound of his own breathing.

"I won't let you leave!" he shouted. "If you don't answer, you're a coward. But I'll expose you!"

He struck a match. The blaze lit the room. There was no one in the room! Raoul locked the door and lit the lights. He opened the closets, the cupboards, hunted around, felt the walls with his moist palms. Nothing!

"I must be going mad," he said aloud, to himself.

He stayed in the room for ten minutes, listening to the gas lights flaring in the silence of the empty room.

He touched nothing, took nothing, not even to remind him of the woman he loved. He left, not knowing what he was doing or where he was going. As he went, an icy draft struck him in the face. He found himself at the bottom of a staircase. Down the stairs behind him came a procession of workers carrying a stretcher covered with a white sheet.

"Which way is out, please," he asked one of the men.

"The door straight in front of you. But let us pass."

Pointing to the stretcher, he asked mechanically, "What is that?"

"*That* is Joseph Buquet, who was found in the third cellar, hanging by his neck among the scenery."

Raoul took off his hat, stepped back to make room for the procession, and went out the open door.

3 *The Mysterious Reason*

Meanwhile, the farewell ceremony for Messieurs Debienne and Poligny was about to take place in the ballet foyer. The two gentlemen, bent on retiring with a grand gesture, had put together a perfect program with the help of all the social figures in Paris.

In the foyer, Sorelli waited for the two retiring managers. She had a glass of champagne in her hand and her speech on the tip of her tongue. The members of the *corps de ballet*, young and old, discussed the day's events with their friends. A few of the dancers had changed clothes, but most still wore their gossamer skirts. All thought to put on a special, solemn face for the occasion; all except little Jammes. At age fifteen, little Jammes seemed to have forgotten the ghost and the death of Joseph Buquet. She chatted and laughed, hopped around and played jokes until the guests of honor appeared. Then Sorelli impatiently hushed her.

Everybody remarked that the retiring managers looked cheerful. The Paris way is to wear a mask of happiness when you are sad, and a sad or bored mask when you are joyful. In Paris, life is a masked ball; the foyer was the last place the two men would betray their sorrow. They were smiling too broadly at Sorelli, who had begun her speech. Suddenly an exclamation from little Jammes broke the smile of the managers and laid bare the worry that lay beneath it.

"The Opera ghost!"

Jammes's voice was terrified. Her finger pointed to

a face that was pale, mournful, and ugly, with two deep black cavities under eyebrows that straddled them.

Everyone laughed, pushed his neighbor at the bar, and wanted to offer the ghost a drink. But he had slipped through the crowd and was gone. Some searched for him, while two elderly gentlemen tried to calm little Jammes and little Giry, who was screaming at the top of her lungs.

Sorelli was furious that she had not been able to finish her speech. The managers kissed and thanked her, and left—followed by the crowd—to repeat the same ceremony on the other floors. They would visit the foyer of the singers, then finally arrive at the top foyer where a supper would be served. Everyone trailed after the managers.

The two new managers received the keys to the Opera doors. These were passed around for examination until someone noticed, seated at the end of the table, the same strange face with the hollow eyes that had caused little Jammes to shout:

"The Opera ghost!"

There he sat, as natural as could be, except that he neither drank nor ate. He did not speak, and no one could remember exactly when he had sat down. The retiring managers' friends thought he was a guest of the new managers, Richard and Moncharmin, while the friends of these two thought he was a guest of the retiring managers Debienne and Poligny. The result was that no one had asked for an explanation, and no one had made any unpleasant remarks or bad jokes to offend the visitor. A few people, unaware of the scene-changer's death, thought the visitor might fit Joseph's Buquet's description of the ghost. But Buquet's ghost had no nose, and this person did. M. Moncharmin describes, in his *Memoirs*, that the guest's nose was "long, thin, and transparent." I would point out that this description might apply to a false nose. Everyone knows that orthopedic science provides beautiful false noses for those who have lost their noses naturally or as the result of an operation.

Messieurs Debienne and Poligny, seated at the center of the table, had not yet seen the man with the death's head. Suddenly he began to speak:

"The ballet girls are right," he said. "The death of poor Buquet is perhaps not so natural as people think."

Debienne and Poligny were startled.

"Buquet is dead?" they cried.

"Yes," replied the man quietly. "He was found this evening, hanging in the third cellar, between a farmhouse set and a scene from *Le Roi de Lahore*."[1]

The two ex-managers stood and stared strangely at the speaker. They were quite excited, more excited that any one should have been, that is, by the announcement of the suicide of a chief scene-changer. They looked at each other; each had turned whiter than the tablecloth. Debienne signaled to Richard and Moncharmin, Poligny muttered a few words of excuse, and all four went into the office. M. Moncharmin, in his *Memoirs*, completes the story:

> MM.[2] Debienne and Poligny got more and more excited, acting as if they had something very difficult to tell us. First they asked if we

---

1. *Le Roi de Lahore* French opera by Jules Massenet (in English, *The King of Lahore*)
2. **MM.** the French abbreviation for *messieurs,* two or more men

knew the man at the table. Then they took the
master keys and advised us to have new locks
made, secretly, for doors we wanted sealed. When
we asked if there were thieves at the Opera, they
replied that there was something worse: *a ghost.*
They told us they would not have mentioned the
ghost, except that the ghost himself had ordered
them to ask us to be pleasant to him and to grant
any request he might make. They said that the
announcement of Buquet's death reminded them
that whenever they disregarded the ghost's wishes something disastrous happened.

During this story, I looked at Richard.
Richard had a reputation for practical jokes, and
he seemed to enjoy what he was hearing as a
joke. He looked serious, nodding his head as the
outgoing managers spoke. But together, we could
not—at the end—help but burst out laughing in
the faces of the two men. They thought we had
gone mad.

Richard asked, half-joking:

"What does this ghost of yours want?"

M. Poligny took out a copy of the lease from
his desk. The Opera lease contains 98 clauses,
ending with four conditions which, if not met,
would be grounds for dismissing a manager. The
copy that M. Poligny produced looked exactly
like ours, except that at the end there was a
paragraph in red ink and a strange handwriting. The paragraph ran:

"5. Or if the manager, in any month, delay for
more than a fortnight[3] the payment of the

---

3. **fortnight** two weeks—a shortened form of "fourteen
nights"

allowance which he shall make to the Opera ghost, an allowance of 20,000 francs a month, say 240,000 francs a year."

"Is that all? Does he want anything else?" asked Richard cooly.

"Yes, he does," replied Poligny.

And he turned over the pages until he found the clause referring to days on which certain boxes were reserved for the president of the republic, the ministers, and so on. Here, a line had been added, also in red ink:

"Box 5 on the grand tier shall be placed at the disposal of the Opera ghost for every performance."

There was nothing left to do but stand up, shake hands with the retiring managers, and congratulate them on their little joke. We commented on the unreasonable attitude of the ghost, and Richard said:

"It seems to me that you were much too kind to the ghost. If I had such a troublesome ghost as this one, I wouldn't hesitate to have him arrested. . . . "

"But how? Where?" they cried in chorus. "We have never seen him!"

"When he comes to the box?"

"*We have never seen him in his box.*"

"Then sell it."

"Sell the Opera ghost's box! Well, gentlemen, you try it!"

At that, we all four left the office. Richard and I had never laughed so much in our lives.

4 *Box 5*

The two new managers of the Opera were quite different in personality. Armand Moncharmin wrote voluminous *Memoirs* while he was co-manager of the Opera. He did not know a note of music, but he was on a first-name basis with influential people in Paris. He was also independently wealthy, charming, and obviously intelligent. He had, after all, selected the best possible partner in Firmin Richard.

Firmin Richard was a composer. He had published pieces of all kinds, and he liked nearly every sort of music and musician. Most musicians felt obliged to like him in return. The only faults one could find with him were that he was a little bossy and he had a quick temper.

The two were so busy enjoying their first few days at the Opera that they forgot all about the ghost. But an incident occurred to prove that the joke—if it was a joke—was not over.

Firmin Richard got to his office that morning at eleven o'clock. His secretary, M. Rémy, gave him several unopened letters marked "Private." One of them caught Richard's eye right away. It was written in red ink and the handwriting seemed familiar to him. It was the red, clumsy writing of the additions in the Opera lease. He opened the letter:

Dear Mr. Manager:
  I am sorry to have to trouble you at a time when you must be very busy, renewing important

engagements, signing fresh ones and generally displaying your excellent taste. I know what you have done for Carlotta, Sorelli, and little Jammes and for a few others whose admirable talent or genius you have suspected.

Of course when I use the terms "talent" and "genius" I do not apply them to Carlotta, who sings like a squirt; nor to Sorelli, who owes her talent to her coaches; nor to little Jammes, who dances like a calf. And I am not speaking of Christine Daaé, either. Though her genius is certain, you jealously prevent her from creating any important roles. But of course you are free to conduct your business as you see fit, aren't you?

I would like to take advantage of the fact that you haven't turned Christine Daaé out onto the streets by asking you to hear her tonight. She will sing the role of Siebel, because she has not been allowed to sing the role of Marguerite since her triumph of the other evening. Also, I must ask you not to sell my box today or any *following days*. I cannot tell you how disagreeably disappointed I was once or twice when I arrived at the Opera to find my box had been sold, at your orders.

I didn't object because, first, I don't like scenes and, second, I thought possibly the former managers, Debienne and Poligny, had neglected to inform you of my little requests. However, I have now received a reply to my letter requesting an explanation from those gentlemen. This reply proves that you know all about my additions to the lease. Consequently, it is clear you are treating me

with outrageous contempt. *If you wish to live in peace, you must not take away my private box.*
Your most obedient and humble servant,
Opera Ghost

With the letter was a clipping from the *Theater Revue*:

O. G.—There is no excuse
for R. and M. We told them
and left your lease in their
hands.
Kind regards.

Firmin Richard had hardly finished reading when Armand Moncharmin came in carrying a similar packet. They looked at each other and burst out laughing.

"They are keeping up the joke," said Richard, "but I don't think it's funny."

"Do they think, just because they have been managers of the Opera, we are going to give them a box forever?" asked Moncharmin.

"I am not in a mood to be laughed at for long," stated Firmin Richard.

"But it's harmless enough," commented Moncharmin. "What do you think they really want? A box for tonight?"

Firmin Richard told his secretary to send tickets for Box 5 on the grand tier to Debienne and Poligny, if it was not already sold. On seeing their addresses, Moncharmin noted that the ghost's letter had been postmarked from Rue des Capucines, which was where Debienne lived.

"You see!" said Richard.

They shrugged their shoulders in regret that two men of that age should be playing such childish tricks.

"Why, those two are jealous!" offered Richard. "But to go to all this time and expense! Have they nothing better to do?"

"They seem to be interested in Christine Daaé," observed Moncharmin.

At that, Richard asked to see the artists who had been waiting to see him for the last two hours. The rest of the day was spent discussing, negotiating, signing, and cancelling contracts. That evening the two tired managers left the Opera without so much as a glance to see if Debienne and Poligny were enjoying the performance.

The next morning the managers received a card of thanks:

Dear Mr. Manager:

Thanks. Charming evening. Daaé exquisite. Choruses need to be waked up. Carlotta commonplace. Will write soon for the 240,000 francs: 233,424 fr. 70 c. to be precise. D. and P. have sent 6,6575 fr. 30 c. for first ten days of allowance for current year. Their privileges ended on the tenth.

Kind regards,
O. G.

There was also a letter from Debienne and Poligny:

Gentlemen:

We are grateful for your kind offer, but you will understand that the idea of hearing *Faust* one more time—as pleasant as it is—cannot make us forget that we have no right to use Box 5 on the grand tier, which belongs exclusively to *him* that we spoke of when we went through the

lease with you last time. See Clause 98, final
paragraph.

Sincerely, etc.

"Those two are beginning to annoy me!" shouted
Richard, grabbing the letter.

That evening Box 5 was sold.

The next morning Richard and Moncharmin
arrived at their offices to find a report written by an
inspector called to Box 5 the night before:

It was necessary to call the municipal officers
twice this evening, to clear Box 5 on the grand
tier, once at the beginning and again in the middle of the second act. The occupants of the box,
who arrived just as the curtain rose for the second act, created a commotion with their laughter
and ridiculous comments. There were cries of
"Hush!" all around them, and the whole house
began to protest when the boxkeeper came to get
me. I entered the box and spoke to the occupants. They did not seem to be in their right
mind, and they made stupid remarks. I said that
if the noise continued I would have to clear the
box. The moment I left, I heard the laughing
again, with fresh protests from the rest of the
audience. I returned with a municipal officer,
who made them leave. They objected, still laughing, saying they would not go unless they had
their money back. Finally they quieted down and
I allowed them to enter the box again. The
laughter began again at once, and this time I
had them ejected.

"Send for the inspector," said Richard to his secretary, who had seen the report and marked it with blue pencil.

Mister Rémy had anticipated the request and called for the inspector right away.

"Tell us what happened," said Richard bluntly.

The inspector stammered and referred to the report.

"But what were those people laughing at?" asked Moncharmin.

"They must have been dining, sir, and seemed more interested in fooling around than in listening to good music. As soon as they entered the box, they came out again and asked the boxkeeper if there was anyone already in the box. 'No,' the woman said. 'Well,' they said, 'when we went in, we heard a voice say *that the box was taken!*'"

"But, when the people arrived, there was no one in the box, was there?" roared Richard.

"Not a soul, sir! And not in the box on the right or in the box on the left! Not a soul, sir, I swear!"

"And what did the boxkeeper say?"

"Oh, she said it was just the Opera ghost."

The inspector grinned. But he soon saw that that was a mistake. The words had no sooner left his mouth than Monsieur Richard became furious.

"Send for the boxkeeper!" he shouted to Rémy. "This minute! And bring her to me here!"

The inspector tried to object, but Richard issued an angry order to keep quiet. When the poor man's lips seemed shut for good, the manager commanded him to open them again.

"Who is the 'Opera ghost'?" he snarled. "Have you ever seen him?"

The inspector was by this time incapable of speech. With a vigorous shake of his head he denied ever having seen the ghost. Having made this response, the inspector thought to leave the room quietly. When Richard looked away to attend to another matter, the inspector sidled toward the door. He was brought up smartly with a thundering:

"Stay where you are!"

The boxkeeper soon arrived, and made herself known to the managers:

"You know me. I'm Mme. Giry.[1] I'm the mother of little Giry, little Meg!" she said in a solemn, proud voice.

Firmin Richard was, for a moment, impressed by her tone, although he did not know Mme., or Giry, or "little" Meg. Then he looked at Mme. Giry, in her faded shawl, worn shoes, old taffeta dress, and dingy bonnet.

"Never heard of her!" he declared. "What happened last night to make you call the municipal officer?"

Mme. Giry turned purple with indignation at his rudeness. She considered just walking out, but changed her mind and said in a haughty voice:

"I'll tell you what happened! The ghost has been annoyed again!"

Seeing that M. Richard was on the verge of losing his temper, M. Moncharmin took over the questioning. Mme. Giry considered it natural for a voice to say the box was taken. She could not explain the phenomenon other than it being the ghost. She had often heard him speak. They could ask anyone, including M. Isadore Saack, who had a leg broken by the ghost. That event, she explained, had also occurred during the former managers' time, in Box 5, and during a performance of *Faust*:

---

1. **Mme.** abbreviation for French title, *Madame,* used before the name or title of a married, or older unmarried, woman

"It was like this, sir. One night M. Maniera and his lady—the jewelers on Rue Mogador—were sitting in the front of the box. Their good friend M. Isadore Saack was sitting behind Mme. Maniera. Méphistophélès[2] was singing when M. Maniera heard a voice in his right ear (his wife was on his left) saying, 'Ha, ha! Julie's not playing at sleeping!' His wife is Julie, so he looks to see who spoke to him. Nobody there! He thinks he must have been dreaming. Then Méphistophélès went on with his serenade. And again M. Maniera hears the voice in his right ear, saying this time, 'Ha, ha! Julie wouldn't mind giving Isadore a kiss!' He turns around again but this time to his left. And he sees his friend Isadore covering his lady's hand with kisses like this"—and she demonstrated with her own palm. "Then they had quite a time! Bang! Bang! M. Maniera, who was big and strong, like you, M. Richard, hit M. Saack, who was small and weak, like you, M. Moncharmin. There was an uproar! People shouted at them to stop. 'Stop them! He'll kill him!' At last M. Isadore Saack managed to run away."

"So the ghost didn't break his leg?" asked Moncharmin, a little annoyed at Mme. Giry's description of his figure.

"He did break it for him, sir," replied Mme. Giry haughtily. "He broke it on the grand staircase, which M. Saack went down too quickly."

"And have you spoken to the ghost, Madame?"

"As clearly as I am now speaking to you, sir!"

"What does he say to you, when he speaks to you?"

"Well, he tells me to bring him a footstool!"

This time, Richard burst out laughing, as did Moncharmin and Rémy, the secretary. Only the

---

2. Méphistophélès the name of the devil in *Faust*

inspector was careful not to laugh. Mme. Giry adopted a threatening attitude.

"Instead of laughing, you'd do better to do as M.
Poligny did—to find out for yourself!" she said
indignantly.

Suddenly she calmed herself, feeling this was a
solemn moment in her life:

"*Look here,*" she said. "They were performing *La
Juive.*[3] Monsieur Poligny decided to watch it from the
ghost's box. I was watching him from the back of the
next box, which was empty. Suddenly, M. Poligny stood
up and walked out stiffly, like a statue. Before I could
speak to him, he was down the staircase, but without
breaking his leg. And from that evening on, no one
tried to take the ghost's box from him. M. Poligny gave
orders that he was to have it for every performance.
And whenever he came, he asked me for a footstool."

"A ghost asking for a footstool! Then this ghost of
yours is a woman?" suggested Moncharmin.

"No, the ghost is a man."

"How do you know?"

"He has a man's voice. This is what happens:
When he arrives, it is usually in the middle of the
first act. He taps three times on the door of Box 5.
The first time I heard those taps, think how puzzled
I was! I knew no one was in the box. I opened the
door, listened, and looked. Nobody! And then I
heard a voice say, 'Mme. Jules'—my poor husband's
name was Jules—a footstool, please.' It made me
feel all-over nervous. But the voice went on, 'Don't be
frightened, Mme. Jules, I am the Opera ghost!' The
voice was so soft and kind that I hardly felt fright-

---

3. *La Juive* French opera by Jacques Halévy (in English,
   The Jewess)

ened. *The voice was sitting in the corner chair, on the right, in the front row."*

"And what did you do?"

"I brought the footstool. Of course, it wasn't for him. It was for his lady! But I never saw her nor heard her."

So now the ghost was married! The two managers noticed the inspector waving his arms to attract their attention. He tapped his forehead to indicate his opinion that Mme. Giry was crazy. The gesture confirmed Richard's decision to get rid of an inspector who kept a lunatic on the payroll. Meanwhile, Madame went on:

"At the end of the performance, he always gives me two francs, sometimes five, sometimes even ten when he hasn't come to a performance for many days. But, since people have begun to annoy him, he gives me nothing at all."

"And how does the ghost manage to give you money?"

"He leaves it on a little shelf in the box. I find the francs with the program, which I always give him. Sometimes I find flowers in the box, a rose that must have dropped from his lady's dress. One day, they left a fan behind."

"And what did you do with it?"

"Well, I brought it back to the box the next night. They took it away with them, and in its place they left me a box of English candy, which I'm fond of."

"That will do, Mme. Giry. You can go."

When Mme. Giry had made a dignified exit, the managers told the inspector they had decided to let the madwoman go. When the inspector left, they instructed the acting-manager to make up *his* last pay, too. Left alone, the two managers talked about what was on their minds. They had both decided they should look into the matter of Box 5 themselves.

5   *The Enchanted Violin*

After the famous night, Christine Daaé did not continue her triumphs right away. She sang only once more at a private function. She turned down an appearance for a charity she had promised to help. She acted as if she was no longer in charge of her own life. She seemed to fear a new triumph.

The Comte de Chagny had tried to use his influence with M. Richard, to please his young brother. Christine wrote to thank him and also to ask him to stop speaking on her behalf. The reason for her strange attitude was not known. Some people saw it as pride; others thought it modesty. But stage people are not as modest as that. I think it would be truthful to attribute her actions to fear. Yes, I think Christine Daaé was frightened by what had happened to her. A letter of Christine's (from the Persian's collection) suggests her dismay:

"I hardly know myself when I sing," she wrote.

Raoul, the Vicomte[1] de Chagny, tried to meet her. In vain he wrote to her, but got no response until one day she sent him a note:

Monsieur:

I have not forgotten the little boy who went into the sea to rescue my scarf. I am writing you

---

1. **Vicomte** French word for *viscount* (pronounced VI-kownt) (This is Raoul's title, a rank below count—Phillippe's rank. In this story both French and English titles are used.)

today, as I am going to Perros to fulfill a sacred duty. Tomorrow is the anniversary of the death of my father, whom you knew and who was very fond of you. He is buried there with his violin, in the graveyard of the little church at the bottom of the hill where we played as children, beside the road where, when we were a little bigger, we said goodbye for the last time.

The Vicomte consulted the railway schedule, dressed quickly, wrote a few lines to be given to his brother, and jumped into a cab. He arrived at the Montparnasse Station just in time to miss the morning train. He waited in poor spirits until the evening train, then he spent the night's ride reading Christine's note over and over again, recalling memories of his childhood. The closer he drew to her, the more fondly he remembered the story of the little Swedish singer. Most of these details are still unknown to the public.

There was once, in a little town near Upsala, in Sweden, a peasant named Daaé who lived with his family. The peasant had a daughter to whom he taught the musical alphabet before she learned to read. Christine's father was a great musician, probably without knowing it. His reputation as a fiddler was widespread, and he was always invited to play for weddings and other festivals. Christine's mother died when she was six. The father, who cared only for his daughter and his music, sold his piece of land and went to Upsala in search of his fortune. He found only poverty.

Returning to the countryside, he wandered from place to place with his daughter, who listened to him happily or sang to his playing. One day Professor

Valérius heard them and took them to Gothenburg. He believed that the father was the finest violinist in the world and that the daughter had the making of a great artist. Christine's education and instruction were provided for. She made rapid progress and charmed everyone with her prettiness, grace, and eagerness to please.

When Valérius and his wife went to France, the Daaés went also. But Mister Daaé was homesick. For hours at a time, he locked himself in his room with his daughter, fiddling and singing very softly. Daaé did not recover his strength until the summer, when the whole family went to Perros-Guirec, in a far corner of Brittany. There the sea was the same color as in his country. He went off with his fiddle, as in the old days, and took his daughter with him. For just a week, they lived as they had when they were so poor in Sweden. They gave the smallest hamlets music to last a year. The people could not understand this rustic fiddler who tramped the roads with a pretty child who sang like an angel. They followed them from village to village.

One day a little boy, out with his governess, made her take a longer walk than normal. He could not tear himself away from the little girl whose pure sweet voice bound him to her. They came to an area that was only sky and sea and a stretch of golden sand. A high wind blew Christine's scarf out to sea. She gave a cry, but the scarf was already far out on the waves. Then she heard a voice say:

"It's all right. I'll go and fetch your scarf out of the sea."

The little boy ran into the sea, dressed as he was, and brought the scarf to her. Boy and scarf were soaked through. The governess made a great fuss, but

Christine laughed and kissed the boy, who was none other than Vicomte Raoul de Chagny, who was staying at Lannion with his aunt.

After that, Daaé gave Raoul violin lessons and the two young friends played together almost every day. A favorite sport was to go like beggars to cottage doors:

"Ma'am," or "Sir . . . have you a little story to tell us, please?"

Most everyone did. Many old Bretons had seen the korrigans[2] dance by moonlight on the heather. A great treat was when Daaé came and sat with them and told this story:

"Little Lottie thought of everything and nothing. Her hair was golden and her soul as clear and blue as her eyes. She was kind to her doll, took care of her clothes and her shoes and her fiddle. Most of all, when she went to sleep, she loved to hear the Angel of Music. . . ."

The Angel of Music played a part in many of Mr. Daaé's stories. Sometimes the Angel leans over a baby's cradle and the child becomes a musical genius. Other times the Angel comes much later because the children are naughty and won't learn their lessons or practice their scales. Still other times he does not come at all, when the children have bad consciences or unkind hearts. No one ever sees the Angel, but he is heard by those who are meant to hear him.

Christine asked her father if he had heard the Angel. Mr. Daaé shook his head sadly, and then his eyes lit up as he said:

"One day *you will*, my child! When I am in Heaven, I will send him to you!"

---

2. **korrigan** fairy sorceress

Three years later, Christine and Raoul met again at Perros. Professor Valérius was dead, but his widow stayed with the Daaés, who continued to play the violin and sing. Raoul was now a young man, and he had come to the shore hoping to find them. Christine and Raoul talked all day. When they left one another, Raoul kissed Christine's hand and said:

"Mademoiselle, I will never forget you!"

He regretted his words because he knew that Christine could not be the wife of the Vicomte de Chagny. As for Christine, she tried to forget him in her devotion to her music. Then her father died, and she seemed to lose her voice, her soul, and her genius. She retained just enough to enter the *conservatoire*,[3] where she did not distinguish herself at all. She took a prize only to please old Madame Valérius, with whom she still lived.

When Raoul saw her at the Opera, he was surprised by the indifference of her singing. He came again and again to hear her. He followed her into the wings. He tried to attract her attention. But she seemed not to see him. She seemed, in fact, not to see anybody. Then came the triumph of the gala performance. The angel's voice, heard upon earth, captured his heart.

But then . . . then there was the man's voice—"You must love me,"—and no one in the room. . . .

Why had she laughed at him? Why did she not recognize him? And why had she now written to him?

At Perros, Raoul walked into the sitting room of the inn, the Setting Sun. Christine stood before him, showing no surprise.

---

3. *conservatoire* school of music, a conservatory

"So you have come," she said. "Someone told me I would find you here when I returned from church."

"Who?" asked Raoul, taking her hand.

"My father, who is dead," she replied.

"Did your father tell you I love you, Christine, and that I can't live without you?"

Christine blushed and turned away. In a trembling voice, she said:

"I did not make you come to tell me such a thing."

"You knew your letter would make me come here. How can you have known that and not know that I loved you?"

"I thought you would remember our childhood games, in which my father often joined. I really don't know what I thought. Perhaps I was wrong to write to you. . . . This anniversary and your appearance the other night in my dressing room reminded me of the time long past. . . ."

There was something unnatural in Christine's attitude. There was sadness and tenderness in her eyes. But why the sadness? He wanted to know that, and he was starting to feel irritated.

"You recognized me in your dressing room, even before I reminded you that I had rescued your scarf from the sea. Why did you pretend not to know me, and why did you laugh?"

Raoul's manner was so rough that Christine stared. Raoul himself was aghast to hear himself starting a quarrel when what he really wanted was to speak words of gentleness and love. But having gone so far, he could only continue:

"You don't answer!" he said angrily and unhappily. "I'll answer for you. There was someone in the room who was in your way."

"If any one was in my way, my friend," replied

Christine coldly, "then it was you, since I had told you to leave the room!"

"So you could be alone with the other!"

"What are you saying?" she asked excitedly. "What 'other' are you talking about?"

"The man to whom you said, 'I sing only for you! . . . tonight I gave you my soul and I am dead!' "

Christine seized Raoul's arm with a surprising strength.

"Then you were listening behind the door! Tell me all you heard!"

"He said, 'Chrisine, you must love me!' "

At the words, a deathly paleness spread over Christine's face. Dark rings formed around her eyes. She staggered and seemed about to faint. Then she recovered a little and said in a low voice:

"Go on!"

"I heard him say, 'Your soul is a beautiful thing, child, and I thank you. No emperor ever received so fair a gift. The angels wept tonight.' "

Christine's eyes stared like a madwoman's. Raoul was terror-stricken. But suddenly her eyes moistened and two giant tears ran down her cheeks. Raoul tried to take her in his arms, but she turned and ran away.

All the next day Christine stayed away from Raoul. He heard she that had had a mass said for her father and that she spent time praying in the the little church. But, Raoul wondered, since she had no more to do at Perros, why did she not go back to Paris?

Raoul walked to the church. Death was all around. Skeletons and skulls by the hundreds were piled against the wall of the church. They were held in place by wire that left the whole gruesome pile visible. Dead people's bones, arranged in rows, like bricks, formed the first layer on which the walls of the sacristy[4] had been built. The door of the sacristy, as in many old Breton churches, opened in the middle of the bony structure.

Raoul said a prayer for Daaé, then he climbed up a slope and sat overlooking the sea. Night fell. He was surrounded by icy darkness, but he did not feel the cold. It was here that he used to come with Christine to see the korrigans dance at the rising of the moon. He had not been able to see them, but Christine, who was a little near-sighted, had claimed to see many. He smiled at the thought, then jumped at a voice behind him:

"Do you think the korrigans will come this evening?"

Raoul tried to speak, but she stopped him.

"I have decided to tell you something serious," Christine said, "very serious. Do you remember the story of the Angel of Music?"

"Of course," he said. "It was here that your father first told it to us."

"And he said, 'When I am in heaven, my child, I will send him to you.' Well, Raoul, my father is in heaven, and I have been visited by the Angel of Music."

"I have no doubt of that," replied the young man seriously. It seemed to him that his friend was only now connecting the memory of her father with the brilliant way she sang at the gala. "No human can sing as you sang the other evening, without the intervention of a miracle. You *have* heard the Angel of Music, Christine."

"You understand it?" she asked, astonished at the

4. **sacristy** room in a church where sacred vessels and clothes are kept and where the clergy dresses

Vicomte's coolness. She brought her face close to his to see his eyes in the darkness. "He comes to give me my lessons every day—*in my dressing room.*"

"In your dressing room?" he echoed stupidly.

"Yes, that is where I have heard him. And you have heard him, too, my friend."

"I? I have heard the Angel of Music?"

"Yes, the other night it was he who was talking when you were listening behind the door. It was he who said, 'You must love me.' But I thought I was the only one to hear his voice. Imagine my astonishment when you told me you could hear him, too!"

Raoul burst out laughing. Christine turned on him with a hostile look.

"Why are you laughing? You think you heard a man, I suppose?"

Raoul's ideas began to get a little confused in the face of Christine's anger.

"*You* think that, Raoul? You, a playmate from my childhood! A friend of my father's! You have changed since those days. What are you thinking of? I am an honest girl, and I don't lock myself up in my room with men. If you had opened the door, you would have seen there was nobody in the room!"

"That's true! I did open the door when you left, and there was no one in the room."

"So, you see! . . . Well?"

"Well, Christine, I think somebody is playing a joke on you."

She gave a cry and ran away. He ran after her, but in a fiercely angry voice she called out: "Leave me! Leave me alone!" And she disappeared.

Raoul returned to the inn very tired and sad. Christine did not come down for dinner. He dined alone, in a gloomy mood. He went to his room and

tried to sleep. There was no sound from Christine's room. The hours passed slowly.

About half past eleven he heard someone moving with a light, stealthy step, in the room next door. So Christine had not gone to bed! Raoul got dressed and waited. His heart pounded when he heard Christine's door open slowly on its hinges. Where could she be going at this hour, when everyone in Perros was fast asleep? Softly opening the door, he saw Christine's small white form slipping down the stairs. Then he heard two voices in rapid conversation. He understood one sentence: "Don't lose the key."

It was the landlady's voice. The door facing the sea was opened, then locked again. Then everything was still.

Raoul ran back into his room and looked out the window. Christine's white form stood on the quay.

The first floor of the Setting Sun was not high. Raoul was able to climb down a tree growing against the wall without disturbing the landlady. Imagine that lady's surprise the next morning when the young man was returned to the inn half frozen and more dead than alive. He had been found, she was told, stretched full length on the steps of the high altar in the little church. She called Christine, who hurried down, and the two women together revived him.

A few weeks later, the tragedy at the Opera caused the police to question the Vicomte de Chagny about events of that night. I quote some of the questions and answers from the official report:

Q. Did Mlle.[5] Daaé not see you come down from

---

5. **Mlle.** abbreviation for French title, *Mademoiselle,* meaning "Miss"

your room by this curious means?

R. No, although walking behind her, I didn't attempt to be quiet. I wanted her to see me. I thought following her this way was unworthy. But she did not. She left the quay and, hearing the church clock strike quarter to twelve, she hurried to the church.

Q. Was there no one in the churchyard?

R. No, and the gate was open.

Q. Could anyone have been hiding behind the tombstones?

R. No. They were very small and partly hidden by snow. It was a very clear night and one could see everything.

Q. What was your frame of mind?

R. Very healthy and peaceful, I assure you. I was concerned at first, but when I saw Mlle. Daaé going to the church, I thought that was natural. I was surprised she didn't hear me behind her. The snow was so hard my footsteps were quite audible. She knelt beside her father's grave and began to pray. Then the clock struck midnight. At the last stroke, she raised her eyes and stretched her arms toward the sky as in ecstasy. I, too, looked up and everything within me was drawn toward the Unseen, *which was playing the most perfect music!*   Christine and I had heard that music as children, but never played so perfectly. If Christine's Angel of Music had existed, he could not have played better on the late musician's violin. When the music stopped, I heard a noise from the heap of skulls. It was as if they were chuckling, and it made me shudder. I thought perhaps some musician was hiding behind the skulls. I wanted to be sure, so I didn't follow Mlle. Daaé when she walked past me toward the gate.

Q. What happened then that you were found in the morning lying half dead on the steps of the altar?

R. First a skull rolled to my feet, then another, and another. It was as if I were the target in a bowling match. Suddenly a shadow glided across the sacristy wall and into the church. I caught a corner of its coat and did not let go. The shadow turned and I saw a terrible death's head that looked at me with scorching eyes. I thought I was face to face with Satan. My heart gave way, and my courage failed me. I don't remember anything else until I awoke the next morning at the Setting Sun.

6 A Visit to Box 5

When we left Firmin Richard and Armand Moncharmin, they were deciding to "look into the little matter of Box 5."

They went down the staircase to the stage, crossed it, went out the subscribers' door, and entered the theater through the first little passageway on the left. They walked through the front row of stalls and looked at Box 5 on the grand tier. They could not see it well because covers had been thrown over the red velvet on the ledges of all the boxes.

Most of the stage hands had gone off for their break, and the two managers were almost alone in the huge, gloomy theater. They made their way through partially completed sets toward the left boxes. Through columns, through balconies of the grand, first, and second tiers they went. The Greek figures in the ceiling watched their progress.

I presume that they were distressed. Moncharmin, in any case, admits in his *Memoirs* that he was impressed:

It may be that the exceptional surroundings in which we found ourselves, in the midst of incredible silence, impressed us to an unusual extent. It may be that the semi-darkness of the theater and the darkness of Box 5 caused a kind of hallucination. At any rate, Richard and I both saw a shape in the box. Neither of us said anything about it, but we seized one another's hand. We

stood like that for some minutes, not moving,
eyes fixed on the same spot. But the shape had
disappeared.

We went out to the lobby to compare impressions of
the 'shape.' Unfortunately, they were not in the least
alike. I had seen something like a death's head resting
on the ledge. Richard had seen an old woman who
looked like Mme. Giry. Laughing like madmen, we ran
to Box 5 on the grand tier, went inside, and found no
shape of any kind.

There is nothing to distinguish Box 5 on the grand
tier from any other boxes. M. Moncharmin and M.
Richard, very amused and laughing at one another,
moved furniture around and lifted cloths and chairs—
particularly the armchair in which the "man's voice"
sat. Altogether the box seemed very ordinary. They
felt the carpet, then went down to the corresponding
box on the tier below. In that Box 5, which is just
inside the first exit from the stalls at the left, there
was also nothing worth mentioning.

"Those people are making fools of us," Richard
exclaimed. "Saturday there will be a performance of
Faust. We'll watch it from Box 5 on the grand tier!"

7 The Fatal Performance

Saturday morning the Opera managers found a letter:

My Dear Managers:
So it is to be war between us?
If you still want peace, here are my four conditions:

1. You must give me back my private box. It is to be free, at my disposal, from now on.

2. The part of Marguerite will be sung tonight by Christine Daaé. Never mind about Carlotta. She will be ill.

3. I absolutely insist that my loyal boxkeeper, Mme. Giry, be rehired immediately.

4. Let me know, by letter handed to Mme. Giry (who will see that it reaches me), that you accept—as your predecessors did—the conditions in the lease regarding my monthly allowance. I will inform you later how to pay it to me.

If you refuse, *Faust* will be performed tonight in a theater with a curse on it.

Take my advice and be warned in time.

O. G.

"Look, I'm getting sick of him, sick!" shouted Richard, banging his fists on his desk.

Just then, Mercier, his acting-manager, entered.

"Lachenel would like to see one of you gentlemen,"

he said. "He says his business is urgent and he seems very upset."

"Who's Lachenel?" asked Richard.

"He's your head groom."

"What do you mean? My head groom?"

"Yes, sir," said Mercier, there are several grooms at the Opera and Lachenel is in charge of them."

"And what does this head groom do?"

"He manages the stable."

"What stable?"

"Yours, sir, the stable of the Opera."

"There's a stable at the Opera? I didn't know that. Where is it?"

"In the cellars, on the Rotunda side. It's a very important department. We have twelve horses for the performances: horses 'used to the boards.' "[1] It is the business of the grooms to teach them. Lachenel is very good at it."

"Very well . . . he can come in."

M. Lachenel came in carrying a riding whip, with which he kept striking his boot in a irritable way.

"Mr. Manager," he said, "I have come to ask you to get rid of all the stablemen."

"How many do you have?" asked Richard.

"Six."

"Six stablemen! That's at least two too many. We don't need more than four for twelve horses."

"Eleven horses," said the head riding master, correcting him.

"Twelve," repeated Richard.

"Eleven," repeated Lachenel. "I did have twelve, but I only have eleven since César was stolen." And he gave himself a good smack on the boot for emphasis.

---

1. **the boards** theatrical term meaning "the stage"

"César has been stolen?" cried the acting-manager. "César, the white horse in *Le Prophète*?[2] How?"

"I don't know. Nobody knows. That's why I want you to sack the whole stable."

"What do your stablemen say?"

"All sorts of nonsense. Some accuse the supervisors. Others pretend it's the acting-manager's doorkeeper."

"But you must have some idea, M. Lachenel," cried Richard.

"Yes. I have," M. Lachenel declared. "I'll tell you what it is. There's no doubt in my mind." He walked closer to the two managers and whispered, "It's the ghost who did the trick!"

Richard jumped.

"What, you too? You too!"

"What do you mean, I too? Isn't it natural, after what I saw?

"What did you see?"

"I saw, as clearly as I now see you, a black shadow riding a white horse that looked exactly like César. I ran after them and I shouted, but they were too fast for me. They disappeared into the underground gallery."

Richard stood up. "You can go, M. Lachenel. We will lodge a complaint against *the ghost*. And we will sack the whole stable."

As soon as M. Lachenel had gone, Richard began foaming at the mouth.

"Prepare that idiot's last paycheck at once, please."

"He's too influential," Mercier ventured.

Moncharmin agreed about the man's influence, not only in government circles but also with the press.

---

2. *Le Prophète* French opera by Giacomo Meyerbeer (in English, *The Prophet*)

"We'd be a laughing stock. We may as well be dead as ridiculous!"

The door opened and Mme. Giry entered, holding a letter in her hand.

"I beg your pardon, but I had this letter from the Opera ghost. He told me to come to you, that you had something . . ."

The poor woman never finished the sentence. She received as unceremonial an exit as Firmin Richard had ever dreamed of giving anyone.

About the same time, Carlotta was brought her letters in bed. Among them there was one anonymous one, in red ink and clumsy handwriting:

If you appear tonight, be prepared for a great misfortune when you open your mouth to sing. It will be a misfortune worse than death.

Carlotta lost her appetite for breakfast. She sat up and thought hard. She had received other letters of this kind, but never one so threatening. Carlotta liked to think that there was a plot against her. She had been jealous of Christine Daaé's successful evening, and she was furious at the good reviews in the newspapers. She put a stop to them immediately, and she did everything she could to smother Christine and cause her unpleasantness. So after thinking carefully about the letter, she decided what to do. Carlotta called all her friends to come to the theater that night. She told them that Christine Daaé had organized a plot against her and that she might need their help.

When M. Richard's private secretary called to inquire about her health, Carlotta said she was well and that, even if she were dying, she would sing the part of Marguerite that evening.

At five o'clock a second anonymous letter arrived. It said simply:

You have a bad cold. If you are wise, you will see that it is madness to try to sing tonight.

Carlotta sang a few notes to reassure herself.

That evening, Carlotta's friends kept their promise and packed the house. The two managers took their places in Box 5.

Vain! In vain do I call, through my vigil weary.
  On creation and its Lord!
Never reply will break the silence dreary!
  No sign! No single word!

Carolus Fonta, the famous tenor, finished Doctor Faust's first appeal to the powers of darkness. Firmin Richard, who was sitting in the ghost's own chair, leaned over to his partner and joked:

"Has the ghost whispered a word in your ear yet?"

"Don't be in such a hurry," answered Armand Moncharmin in the same tone. "The performance has just begun. Remember the ghost does not usually come until the middle of the first act."

The first act ended without incident. The managers looked at each other when the curtain fell.

"The ghost is late," Richard noted.

"It's not a bad audience, for a theater with a curse on it," commented Moncharmin. Then he noticed a fat, rather vulgar-looking woman dressed in black, sitting in a stall in the middle of the theater. There was a man on each side of her. "Who are *those*?" asked Moncharmin.

"*Those* are my concierge,[3] her husband and her brother. She has never been to the Opera; this is the first time. And since she will be here every night, I wanted her to have a good seat before spending her time showing other people to theirs."

Richard explained that he had persuaded his concierge to take Mme. Giry's place. He wanted to see if this woman would be intimidated by Box 5 the way the old lunatic was.

The ghost! Moncharmin had forgotten about him, particularly since he had not made an appearance. Moncharmin was about to say so, when their stage manager burst through the door of the box.

"What's the matter?" both asked, surprised to see the manager there at such a time.

"Carlotta's furious. It seems there's been a plot cooked up by Christine Daaé's friends."

"What on earth . . .?" began Richard. But then the curtain rose for the second act, so he motioned the stage manager away.

"Then Daaé has friends?" asked Moncharmin.

"Yes, she has. Across there," he said, pointing to a box on the grand tier that contained only two men.

"The Comte de Chagny?"

"Yes, he spoke to me in support of her so enthusiastically that, if I didn't know he was Sorelli's friend . . ."

"Really? Really?" said Moncharmin. "And who is the pale young man beside him?"

"That's his brother, the viscount."

"He should be in his bed. He looks ill."

The stage rang with music.

---

3. **concierge** person who lives in an apartment building and serves as a doorkeeper, manager, and janitor for the building

Red or white liquor,
Coarse or fine!
What can it matter,
So we have wine?

The dancers—students, citizens, soldiers, girls, and women—whirled. Christine Daaé made her entrance as Siebel. Carlotta's friends expected some outburst, but nothing happened.

By contrast, Carlotta crossed the stage and sang the only two lines Marguerite had in the second act:

No, my lord, not a lady am I, nor yet a beauty,
And do not need an arm to help me on my way.

Her friends responded with applause that was so enthusiastic and uncalled for that people in the audience stared at one another in confusion. Other than that, the second act also finished without incident.

The managers left the box to see what the so-called plot against Carlotta was about. But they soon returned to the box, having dismissed it as a rumor.

The first thing they saw, when they entered the box, was a box of English candy on the ledge shelf. They asked who had put it there. No one knew. When they went back in again, they found next to the candy—opera glasses. They looked at one another. They had no desire to laugh. Everything Mme. Giry had told them came to mind, and then . . . and then . . . they felt a strange draft around them. They sat down in silence.

The next scene was in Marguerite's garden:

Gentle flow'rs in the dew,
Be message from me . . .

As she sang these lines, holding roses and lilacs, Christine saw the Vicomte de Chagny in his box. For a moment, her voice seemed less sure and less crystal-clear than usual. Something seemed to deaden her singing.

The viscount put his head in his hands and wept. The count, behind him, was very angry. He had seen his brother return from a mysterious journey in a terrible state. Raoul's explanation had been unsatisfactory, and the count had asked Christine for an appointment. She had actually replied that she could not see him or his brother. . . .

> *Would she but deign to hear me*
> *And with one smile to cheer me . . .*

Raoul thought about the letter he had received on his return to Paris. Christine had arrived before him.

> My Dear Little Playmate:
> You must have the courage not to see me again, and not to speak of me again. If you love me just a little, do this for me. I will never forget you, dear Raoul. Your life depends on it.
>   Your Little Christine

Carlotta as Marguerite made her entrance to thunderous applause.

> *I wish I could but know who was he*
> *That addressed me,*
> *If he was noble or, at least, what his name is . . .*

When Marguerite finished singing she was cheered

loudly. She was cheered again when she came to the end of the Jewel Song:

> *Ah, the joy of past compare*
> *These jewels bright to wear!* . . .

Carlotta felt very sure of herself. She threw herself into the part. She seemed about to have a new success, when suddenly . . . a terrible thing happened.

As Faust, kneeling, sang of love:

> *Let me gaze on the form below me* . . .
> *To love thy beauty to!*

And Marguerite replied:

> *Oh, how strange!*
> *Like a spell does the evening bind me!*. . .

At that moment, the terrible thing happened. Carlotta croaked like a frog:

"Co-ack!"

Everyone was horrified—Carlotta, the entire audience. The two managers could not control an exclamation. It was not natural. Everyone felt there was witchcraft behind it. Poor, wretched, crushed Carlotta! If it had been anybody but Carlotta, the audience would have hooted. But everyone knew what a perfect instrument her voice was.

Carlotta tried to persuade herself that it had not happened. She was the victim of an illusion, an illusion of the ear, not her voice betraying her. . . .

Meanwhile in Box 5, the two managers had paled. They were filled with dread. They had fallen within the influence of the ghost. They had felt his breath.

Moncharmin's hair stood on end. Richard perspired. The ghost was all around them, behind them, beside them. They felt his presence without seeing him. They heard his breath close, close, close to them. They were sure that there were three people in the box. They trembled. . . . They thought about running away. . . . They dared not. . . . They dared not move. . . . What was going to happen?

This happened:

"Co-ack!"

The theater had a curse on it! The ghost had told them a catastrophe would come! Richard's stifled voice was heard calling to Carlotta to go on. Her voice once more filled the house:

> *I feel without alarm . . .*
> *I feel without alarm*—co-ack!
> *With its melody enwind me*—co-ack!
> *And all my heart sub*—co-ack!

The house was in an uproar. The managers collapsed in their chairs. They did not dare turn around; the ghost was chuckling behind their backs! At last, they clearly heard his voice in their right ears. The impossible voice, the mouth-less voice, saying:

She is singing tonight to bring the chandelier down!

As one, they raised their eyes to the ceiling and uttered a terrible cry. The immense chandelier was slipping down, coming toward them, at the call of the ghost's voice. Its hook released, it plunged toward the ground, smashing into the middle of the stalls. There were a thousand shouts of terror and a wild rush for the doors.

The newspapers wrote that many were injured and one killed. That victim was a poor woman who had come to the Opera for the first time in her life. It was said that she knew M. Richard and that she had come to the performance with her husband and her son. She died on the spot. The next morning, a newspaper appeared with this headline as her sole epitaph:

ONE THOUSAND KILOS ON THE HEAD OF A CONCIERGE!

8   *The Mysterious Brougham*

The evening was tragic for all concerned. Carlotta fell ill. As for Christine Daaé, she disappeared after the performance. A fortnight passed without her being seen at the Opera or outside it.

Raoul tried to find her. He wrote to her at Mme. Valérius' house and got no reply. One afternoon he went to the managers' office to ask about her. He found both managers looking extremely worried. They had lost all their spirit. They were seen crossing the stage with hanging heads, pale cheeks, and worried brows, as though followed by some terrible thought.

They had difficulty speaking about the chandelier. The inquest ended with a verdict of accidental death, caused by wear and tear on the chains by which the chandelier hung.

In their daily routines, they were impatient with everybody except Mme. Giry, who had been reinstated in her prior job. When the Vicomte de Chagny inquired about Christine, they told him she was on holiday. Mlle. Daaé had, they said, asked for a leave of absence for health reasons.

Raoul decided to go to see Mme. Valérius. He remembered what he had seen at Perros. Christine was imaginative and naive. Her education had been filled with legends. She constantly brooded over her father. She was easily swept into a state of ecstasy at the sound of certain music. Yes, Raoul was sure that she could very easily fall prey to some mysterious and unscrupulous trickster. But who? Raoul asked himself that question as he hurried off to see Mamma Valérius.

Raoul was ushered into a room where he recognized the kind face of Christine's guardian. Mama Valérius' hair was quite white, but her eyes had not aged.

"Madame . . . where is Christine?" he asked at once.

And the old lady replied calmly:

"She is with her good genius!"

"What good genius?" exclaimed Raoul.

"Why, the Angel of Music! You must not tell anybody," said the old woman. She smiled at him and put her finger to her lips, warning him to be still.

"You can rely on me," said Raoul, hardly knowing what he was saying.

"I know I can!" she said with a happy laugh. "But come near me as you used to do when you were a little boy. Give me your hands, as you did when you brought me the story of little Lotte. I am very fond of you, M. Raoul, you know. And Christine is too!"

The young man sighed and had trouble collecting his thoughts. He asked in a low voice: "What makes you think she is fond of me, madame?"

"She used to talk about you every day."

'And what did she tell you?"

"She told me you had made her a proposal!" laughed the old lady heartily.

Raoul sprang from his chair, blushing furiously.

"What's this? Where are you going? Sit down, please. Do you think I will let you leave this way? If you're angry with me for laughing, I am sorry. After all, what has happened is not your fault. Didn't you know? . . . Did you think Christine was free? Christine couldn't marry, even if she wanted to!"

"But I don't know anything about that! . . . Why can't Christine marry?"

"Because of the Angel of Music, of course. He forbids her to marry!"

"The Angel of Music forbids her to marry!"

"Oh, yes . . . without telling her as much, of course. It's like this: he tells her that she would never hear him again if she married. That's all. So you understand she can't let the Angel of Music go. I thought Christine had told you all this when she met you at Perros. She went there with her good genius."

"She went to Perros with her good genius, did she?"

"He arranged to meet her there, at her father's grave in the churchyard. He promised to play her *The Resurrection of Lazarus* on her father's violin!"

Raoul tore at his gloves in fury.

"How long has Christine known this 'genius'?"

"About three months . . . Yes, three months since he began to give her lessons."

The young viscount threw up his hands.

"Where, may I ask?"

"Now that she has gone away with him, I don't know. But before that, it was in Christine's dressing room. It would be impossible here. But in the Opera at eight o'clock in the morning, no one is there to hear, do you see?"

"Yes, I see! I see !" he cried and rushed out. When he got home he collapsed. His brother asked for no explanation. But he told Raoul that Christine had been seen with a man in the Boulogne Park. She had been seen driving in a brougham[1] with the window down. She seemed to be taking in the night air. There was a full moon, and she was recognized beyond a doubt. As for her companion, only his shadowy outline

---

1. **brougham** light, closed carriage drawn by one horse — the driver sits outside in front

could be seen leaning back in the dark. The carriage proceeded slowly along the road behind the grandstand at Longchamp race course.

That night at ten o'clock Raoul found himself alone, in a taxicab, behind the race course. It was bitter cold. He told the driver to wait for him at the corner. He hid himself as well as he could, and stamped his feet to keep warm. After about thirty minutes a carriage turned the corner of the road and came in his direction very slowly.

As it approached, he saw a woman leaning her head from the window. The moonlight shed a gleam over her features.

"Christine," he shouted without intending to.

He wished he had not, because immediately the carriage window was closed. The brougham rushed past him before he had a chance to react. It soon was only a dot on the white road.

His heart was cold as he stared down the road. She had trifled with him. She covered herself modestly in order to pass with her mysterious lover! Surely there must be a limit to the lies! . . . He wanted to die, and at twenty years old!

His valet found him in the morning sitting on the bed, not undressed from the evening before. Raoul grabbed the mail from his hands. He had recognized Christine's paper and handwriting. The note read:

Dear:

Go to the masked ball at the Opera the night after tomorrow. At midnight, be in the little room behind the chimney place. Stand near the door leading to the Rotunda.[2] Don't mention this to

---

2. **Rotunda** round hall or room

anyone on earth. Wear a white domino[3] and be carefully masked. As you love me, do not let anyone recognize you.

Christine

---

3. **domino** large, full-length cape with a hood

9 *At the Masked Ball*

The envelope was covered with mud, and it was unstamped. It had been thrown out of a window in the hopes that someone would pick it up and deliver it, which is what had happened.

Raoul was torn. Was she an unfortunate, innocent young woman? A victim? A prisoner? What monster had carried her off, and how? But then Raoul remembered the Angel of Music. . . . For three months he had been giving her lessons. Now he was taking her for drives in the park! What games was she playing? She was taking advantage of his good nature and youth! Raoul's thoughts flew from one extreme to the other. He did not know whether to curse Christine or pity her. In any event, he bought a white domino costume.

The ball was attended by a large number of artists, with their models and students. Raoul climbed the staircase shortly before twelve. He paid no attention to the crowds laughing and dancing. He found the room mentioned in the letter, but it, too, was crammed.

Raoul leaned against the doorjamb and waited, but not for long. Someone in a black domino costume passed by and squeezed the tips of his fingers. He understood it was Christine and followed her.

"Is that you Christine?" he asked through clenched teeth.

She raised a finger to her lips, to warn him to be silent. Raoul followed her without speaking. He was afraid of losing her. His feelings of mistrust were gone.

He was ready to show forgiveness. He was in love, and he knew she would be able to explain her curious actions.

The black domino looked back from time to time to see if the white domino was still following. Once more Raoul passed through the great hall. This time he noticed a group crowding around someone whose strange appearance was causing a sensation. It was a man dressed all in red, with a huge hat and feathers on top of a death's head. From his shoulders hung an immense red velvet cloak which trailed along the floor. It was embroidered with some words, which everyone read and repeated aloud, "Don't touch me! I am Red Death stalking abroad!"

One man did try to touch him. A skeleton hand shot out and violently seized the man's wrist. The man, feeling the crush of knucklebones, let out a cry of pain and terror. When the Red Death finally let him go, the man fled.

Just at that moment Raoul passed by. He nearly spoke aloud:

"The Death's Head of Perros!"

He had recognized the figure! He started to follow the man in red, forgetting Christine. But the black domino grabbed his arm and pulled him from the room where the Red Death was stalking.

The black domino kept looking back. Twice she seemed to see something that startled her. She quickened her pace as though fearful of being followed.

They went up two floors. Here the stairs and corridors were almost deserted. The black domino opened the door of a private box and motioned the white domino to follow. Then Christine whispered to him to stay at the back of the box. Raoul removed his mask. Christine kept hers on. She put her ear to the door and listened for a sound. She opened the door and looked into the corridor. In a low voice, she said:

"He must have gone up higher." Then suddenly: "He's coming down again!"

She tried to close the door, but Raoul held it open. On the top step of the staircase he saw *a red foot*, followed by another. Slowly the whole red robe of the Red Death met his eyes. And he once more saw the death's head of Perros. Raoul was on the verge of rushing out, but Christine slammed the door shut. She held him back with unexpected strength.

"It's he!" cried Raoul. "The man who hides behind that hideous mask of death! He's the evil genius from the churchyard at Perros! . . . Red Death! . . . He is your friend . . . your Angel of Music! But I will snatch off his mask and my own, and this time we will look one another in the eye. There will be no lies between us, and I will find out whom you love and who loves you!"

Christine flung out her arms against the door, and said:

"In the name of our love, Raoul, I will not let you pass!"

He stopped. . . . In the name of their love? . . . She had never said she loved him. . . . Her object must be to gain some time. . . . She wanted to give the Red Death time to escape. . . . In a voice of childish hatred, he said:

"You lie. You don't love me. You never loved me! I let you make fun of me! Why did you let me hope? I am an honest man, and I believed you were an honest woman. But your only intention was to deceive me. You've deceived us all! You've taken advantage of your guardian, who still believes in you while you go around the Opera Ball with the Red Death! . . . I hate you. . . ."

"One day, Raoul, you will beg my forgiveness for all those ugly words. And when you do, I'll forgive you!"

"I shall go mad! I shall die of shame!"

"No, dear, live!" said Christine in a changed voice. "And goodbye, Raoul. You will never see me again."

"Where he is taking you? To what hell? . . . or what paradise?"

"I came here tonight to tell you that, but I cannot now. You would not believe me! You have lost faith in me, Raoul. It is finished!"

She spoke in such a sad tone that the young man began to be sorry for his cruelty.

"But look here!" he cried. "Tell me what all this means. You're free. You come here, you go around Paris. Why not go home? What is this story about the Angel of Music you told Mme. Valérius? You seem sensible, Christine. You know what you are doing. And meanwhile your guardian waits for you at home and appeals to your 'good genius.' Explain yourself, Christine. Anyone would be as deceived as I was. What is this farce?"

Christine simply took off her mask and said: "Dear, it is a tragedy!"

Raoul now saw her face. The fresh complexion of former days was gone. A deathly pallor covered her features, and dark circles surrounded her eyes. Raoul was shocked.

"Christine, please forgive me!" he moaned. "You said you would forgive me. . . ."

"One day, perhaps!" she said putting on her mask. And she walked away. When he tried to follow, she forbade him with a firm gesture.

He watched her until she was out of sight. Then he went down among the crowd, hardly knowing where he was going. His footsteps took him to Christine's dressing room, the room where he had first begun to suffer. He tapped at the door. No answer. He entered the dressing room, as he had when he looked for "the man's voice." The room was empty. He saw writing paper on a little desk. He was thinking of writing Christine, when he heard steps in the hallway. He had only time to hide in the inner room which was separated by a curtain.

Christine entered with a tired movement. She sighed and let her head fall into her two hands. Raoul heard her murmur: "Poor Erik!"

Who was Erik, and why would she pity him? It was Raoul who was unhappy!

Christine began to write, calmly and deliberately She wrote and wrote, filling two, three, four pages. Suddenly she raised her head and hid the sheets. She seemed to be listening. Raoul listened, too. There was a strange sound, a distant rhythm. A faint singing came from the walls. The song became plainer. . . the words became clear . . . he heard a beautiful, soft voice . . . but a male voice. . . . The voice came nearer . . . through the wall. . . . It was now *in the room* . . . in front of Christine.

Christine stood and addressed the voice:

"Here I am, Erik. I'm ready. But you are late."

The voice without a body sang on. Raoul had never in his life heard anything more beautiful, more glorious, more powerful, more triumphant. He began to understand how, under its influence, Christine Daaé had been able to perform superhumanly before a stunned audience.

The voice was singing the Wedding-Night Song from *Roméo et Juliette*. The strains went through Raoul's heart. He drew back the curtain and walked to where Christine stood against the mirror.

Fate links thee to me for ever and a day!

Christine walked toward her image in the glass and the image came toward her. The two Christines—the real and the reflection—touched. Raoul put out his arms to hold the two in an embrace. But suddenly he was flung staggering back, and an icy blast swept over his face. He saw, not two, but four, eight, twenty Christines spinning around him, laughing and fleeing so swiftly he could not touch them. At last everything stood still, and he saw himself in the glass. But Christine had disappeared.

He touched the glass, the walls. Nothing. The room still echoed with the singing:

Fate links thee to me for ever and a day!

Which way had Christine gone? Which way would she return? Would she return? She had declared that everything was finished. And the voice was repeating:

Fate links thee to me for ever and a day!

Thee to me? To whom?

Worn out, beaten, he sat on the chair Christine had left. Like her, he let his head fall into his hands, and he wept. He wept the hot, heavy tears of a jealous child and the tears of real sorrow, as do all lovers on earth, a sorrow that he expressed aloud:

"Who is this Erik?"

10 *"Forget the Man's Voice"*

The day after Christine vanished, Raoul went to call on Mme. Valérius. He was surprised but delighted to find Christine seated at the bedside of the old woman, who was sitting up knitting. The color had returned to the young woman's cheeks. The dark circles around her eyes had disappeared.

She stood up, showing no emotion and offered her hand.

"Well, M. de Chagny," exclaimed Mamma Valérius, "don't you know our Christine? Her good genius has sent her back to us!"

"Mamma!" Christine broke in promptly, "I thought there was to be no more question of that! You know there is no such thing as the Angel of Music!"

"But he gave you lessons for three months!"

"Mamma, I have promised to explain everything to you one day. But you have promised me, until that day, to ask no more questions whatsoever!"

"Provided *you* have promised never to leave me again, Christine. But *have* you promised that?"

Raoul interrupted:

"There is *one* thing you must promise, Christine. It is the only thing that will reassure your adopted mother and me. We will not ask a single question about the past if you promise us to remain under our protection in the future."

"That is a promise I refuse to make to you!" Christine said haughtily. "You have no right to control me. There is only one man in the world who has the right to ask an account of my actions: my husband! Well, I am not married and I never plan to marry!"

She threw out her hands to emphasize her point. Raoul turned pale, not only at her words, but because he had caught sight of a plain gold band on Christine's finger.

"You have no husband, but you wear a wedding ring."

He tried to take her hand, but she drew back swiftly.

"That is a present!" she said, trying to hide her embarassment.

"Christine, why deceive us further? That ring is a promise, and a promise accepted! Christine, I am alarmed for you. You are under a very dangerous spell. I heard the voice. It is a very dangerous voice. Christine, in the name of Heaven, in the name of your father who is in Heaven now and who loved you so dearly and who loved me, too, tell us to whom that voice belongs. If you do, we will save you, your guardian and I, in spite of yourself! Come, Christine, the name of the man! The name of the man who put that ring on your finger!"

"Monsieur de Chagny," the young woman declared coldly, "you will never know. How can you condemn a man whom you have never seen, whom no one knows, and about whom you know nothing?"

"Christine, I know the name you thought to keep from me forever. . . . The name of your Angel of Music, mademoiselle, is Erik!"

Christine turned white as a sheet and stammered: "Who told you?"

"You told me yourself."

"How? . . . When? . . ."

"When you went to your dressing room the other

night, you said, 'Poor Erik'! Well, Christine, there was a poor Raoul who overheard you."

"Oh, you unhappy man!" moaned the young woman, showing signs of terror. "Unhappy man! Do you want to die?"

"Perhaps."

Raoul said the "perhaps" with so much love and despair that Christine let out a sob. She took his hands and looked at him with pure affection:

"Raoul," she said, "forget *the man's voice* and do not remember his name. You must never try to understand the mystery of *the man's voice!*"

"Is the mystery so terrible?"

"It is the most awful mystery on this earth. Swear to me that you will not try to find out," she insisted. "Swear to me that you will never come to my dressing room again, unless I send for you."

"Then you will send for me sometimes, Christine?"

"I promise."

"When?"

"Tomorrow."

"Then I will do as you ask."

He went away, cursing Erik and resolving to be patient.

11   *Above the Trapdoors*

The next day, Raoul saw Christine at the Opera. She was still wearing the plain gold ring, but she was kind to him. They talked about the plans he was making for his future, for his career.

He told her that his Polar expedition was to start in a month. She suggested he should consider the voyage as a step toward fame. When he replied that fame without love had no appeal for him, she treated him like a child who would get over his sorrow quickly. But she seemed to be thinking of something, some new thing that had just entered her mind. Her eyes glowed with it.

"What are you thinking, Christine?"

"I am thinking in a month we shall have to say goodbye forever. And that we shall never be married: that is understood."

She clapped her hands with glee. Raoul stared at her in amazement.

"But," she continued, giving her two hands to Raoul as if they were a present, "if we can't be married, we can . . . we can be engaged! Nobody will know but us, Raoul. We can be engaged for a month! In a month, you will go away, and I can be happy at the thought of that month all my life!"

She was happy with her inspiration. Then she became serious again:

"This," she said, "is *a happiness that will harm no one.*"

Raoul jumped at the idea.

"Mademoiselle, I have the honor to ask for your hand."

"You already have both of them my dear! Raoul, we will be very happy."

It was a game, and they enjoyed it as the children they were. But one day, about a week after the game began, Raoul's heart was sad. He stopped playing and uttered these wild words:

"I won't go to the North Pole!"

Christine had not dreamed this could happen. It showed her how dangerous the game could be. She said nothing and went straight home.

That evening Christine did not sing. And Raoul did not receive his daily letter. The next morning he went to Mamma Valérius, who told him Christine had gone away for two days.

Christine returned the following day. She returned in triumph. She sang as she had for the gala performance and received thunderous applause.

The viscount, of course, was present. He was the only one to suffer on hearing the applause, for Christine still wore the plain gold ring. And a distant voice whispered in the young man's ear:

"She is wearing the ring, and you did not give it to her. She gave her soul tonight, and she did not give it to you. If she will not tell you what she was doing these two days, go and ask Erik!"

He ran back stage. Christine was looking for him and saw him right away. She said:

"Quick! Quick! . . . Come here!"

And she pulled him along to her dressing room.

Immediately, Raoul threw himself on his knees. He swore he would go on the voyage, and begged her not to go away again. They kissed like a brother and sister who have suffered a common loss and meet to mourn a dead parent.

Suddenly, she jumped away and seemed to listen to something. Pointing to the door, she said:

"Tomorrow, my betrothed. And be happy, Raoul. Tonight I sang for you."

He returned the next day, but the two days absence had broken the spell of their make-believe. They exchanged sad looks without saying anything. Christine took Raoul to the stage and made him sit on the wooden curb of a well on the set for the evening's performance.

On another day, she wandered through the gardens with him. She dragged him up above the stage: along bridges, among pulleys and ropes. She took him to the wardrobe and property rooms. She took him all over her empire, which was artificial but immense. It covered seventeen stories and was inhabited by an army of subjects. She walked among them like a queen: talking, encouraging, asking, giving advice. They all knew her, and they loved her because she was interested in their troubles and work.

She knew hidden corners that were secretly inhabited by little old couples. She knocked on their doors and introduced Raoul to them as Prince Charming. They told the young couple legends of the Opera. They knew nothing of outside the Opera. They had lived there for years without number. Management had forgotten all about them; the history of France had run its course unknown to them. Nobody remembered they existed.

Days passed with these adventures. Then Christine began to become more and more nervous. On their walks, she would suddenly start to run with no reason or else suddenly stop. Her hand, turned ice-cold in an instant, held him back. Sometimes her eyes pursued imaginary shadows. She would laugh a breathless laugh that often became tears. When Raoul tried to speak, she would answer feverishly:

"It is nothing. . . . I swear it is nothing."

Once, when they passed over an open trap door on the stage, Raoul asked:

"You have shown me the upper part of your empire, Christine, but there are strange stories told of the lower part. Shall we go down?"

"Never! . . . I will not have you go there! Besides, it's not mine . . . *everything that is underground belongs to him!*"

And she dragged him away. Suddenly the trap door was closed quickly. They were dazed.

"Perhaps *he* was there," Raoul said, at last.

"No, no, it was the door-shutters. He has shut himself up; he is working." She shivered.

"What is he working at?"

"Oh, something terrible! But all the better for us. When he's working at it, he sees nothing. He does not eat or drink or breathe for days and nights at a time. He becomes a living dead man and has no time to amuse himself with the trapdoors."

On the next day and those following, Christine was careful to avoid the trapdoors. Her nervousness increased. One day she arrived very late, with her face pale and her eyes very red. Raoul blurted out that he would not go on the North Pole expedition unless she told him the secret of the man's voice.

"I will remove you from his power, Christine. I swear I will. And you won't have to think of him any more."

"Is it possible?" She asked this as she dragged Raoul up to the top floor of the theater, far from the trapdoors.

"I'll hide you in some unknown corner of the world, where *he* can not come looking for you. You'll be safe, and then I'll go away. . . since you've sworn not to marry."

Christine seized Raoul's hands and squeezed them. But suddenly she was alarmed again:

"Higher!" was all she said. "Higher still!"

Despite the care Christine took to look behind her at every moment, she failed to see the shadow that followed her like her own shadow. It stopped when she stopped. It started again when she did, and it made no noise. As for Raoul, he saw nothing either. Christine was in front of him, so nothing that happened behind was of any interest.

12 *Apollo's Lyre*

They reached the roof with its three domes. All of Paris was at work below. Christine and Raoul walked close together around the roof.

The shadow had followed behind them, clinging to their steps. The two young people did not suspect its presence. They finally sat down under the great bronze statue of Apollo lifting his lyre[1] to a crimson sky.

It was a gorgeous spring evening. Clouds gathered brilliant colors from the setting sun. Gold and purple, they drifted by. Christine said:

"Soon we'll go farther and faster than the clouds. We'll go to the end of the world, and then you'll leave me. But, Raoul, when the moment comes for you to take me away, if I refuse to go with you—you must carry me off by force!"

"Are you afraid you will change your mind, Christine?"

I don't know," she said, shaking her head oddly. "If I don't go back to him, terrible things may happen! . . . But I can't go back, I can't do it! . . . I know I should feel sorry for people who live underground . . . but he is too horrible! I have only one day left. If I don't go, he will come and drag me with him, underground. And he will tell me on his knees that he loves me! He will cry, with his death's head. Those tears, Raoul, in the black

---

1. **lyre** small harp used in ancient Greece to accompany singers and reciters

eyesockets of the death's head—I can't bear to see those tears again!"

"Let's go, Christine. Let's go now, at once!"

He tried to drag her away, then and there. But she stopped him.

"No, no," she said, shaking her head sadly. "Not now. It would be too cruel. Let him hear me sing tomorrow evening. Then we'll go away. Come to my dressing room at midnight exactly. He'll be waiting for me in the dining room by the lake. Promise me that, if I refuse, you'll take me away by force. I fear that if I go back this time, I won't ever return."

She sighed, and there seemed to be another sigh behind her.

"Did you hear something?" Her teeth chattered.

"No," said Raoul, "I heard nothing."

"It is too terrible to be always trembling like this! I know we are not in danger here in the sunlight. Birds of the night cannot bear to look at the sun. I have never seen him by daylight . . . it must be awful!. . . . The first time I saw him I thought he would die!"

"Why?" asked Raoul, a little frightened at the turn this conversation had taken.

"Because I had seen him!"

This time both Raoul and Christine turned around.

"There is someone in pain," said Raoul. "Did you hear?"

They stood up and looked around the roof. They were quite alone.

"Tell me how you saw him first."

"I heard him for three months before I saw him. The first time I heard him, I thought it was someone singing in another room. But there was no voice outside, only in my room. And it not only sang, it spoke to me and answered my questions. I had never received the Angel of Music that my father promised to send me as soon as he died. So I asked the man's voice and it said, yes, it was the Angel's voice, the voice I was expecting, and which my father had promised. From that time on, the voice and I became good friends. It offered to give me lessons every day. I agreed and kept my appointment every day. *You* have no idea, even though you have heard the voice, what those lessons were like.

"No, I don't. What was your accompaniment?" asked Raoul.

"We were accompanied by a music I don't know. It was behind the wall and extremely accurate. I hardly knew my own voice when I sang. It was frightening. At the voice's request, my progress was a secret between the two of us and Mamma Valérius. Outside the room I sang with my ordinary voice. No one noticed. I did everything the voice said. I waited and lived in this sort of dream. It was then that I saw you in the audience. I was so glad I showed my delight when I reached my dressing room. Unfortunately, the voice soon asked the reason for my delight. I told it and it fell silent. I called to it, but there was no reply. I begged it to talk to me, but nothing! I was afraid it was gone for good. That night I went home in a terrible state. When I told Mamma Valérius, she said 'Why, of course the voice is jealous.' That was when I realized that I loved you!"

Christine stopped and laid her head on Raoul's shoulder. They did not see the movement a few feet away from them. It was the creeping shadow of two great black wings, a shadow coming so near that it could have smothered them by closing over them.

"The next day," Christine continued, "the voice was there in the dressing room. It spoke very sadly. It told me that, if I gave my heart here on earth, there was nothing for the voice to do but to go back to Heaven. I was terrified I might never hear it again. I thought about my love for you and I saw the danger in it. I didn't even know if you remembered me. In any event, your position in society meant there was no possibility of marriage between us. So I swore to the voice that you were like a brother to me. I said my heart was incapable of earthly love. That is why, dear, I refused to recognize you whenever I saw you on the stage or in the corridors. Meanwhile, the lessons were frenzied, until one day the voice said, 'You are now ready, Christine Daaé, to give a little of the music of Heaven.' I don't know why Carlotta was absent that night, and I don't know why I was selected to sing in her place. But I sang with a rapture I had never known before. I felt for a moment like my soul was leaving my body."

"Oh, Christine," said Raoul. "I saw the tears stream down your cheeks. How could you sing like that while crying?"

"I felt myself faint," said Christine, "and I saw you by my side. But the voice was there, too. I was afraid for you, so I pretended not to recognize you. . . . But there was no fooling the voice. The voice recognized you and it was jealous! . . . It said that I did not treat you like a brother. I said to the voice, 'I am going to Perros tomorrow and I am asking Raoul de Chagny to go with me.' 'Do as you please,' the voice said. 'But I will be at Perros, too. I go wherever you go, Christine. And if you have not lied to me, I will play something for you—*The Resurrection of Lazarus*, on your father's violin, at your father's tomb, at the stroke of midnight.' That, Raoul, is when I wrote you to come to Perros. How could I have been so deceived? How could I have failed to see the human selfishness behind the voice's actions? I had come so far under his control!"

"But you *did* come to know the truth, after all!" cried Raoul.

"Know the truth, Raoul? Do you remember that tragic night when Carlotta croaked like a frog? When the chandelier crashed to the floor? There were people killed and wounded that night. My first thought was for you and the voice. I knew *you* were all right because I had seen you in your brother's box. But the voice told me it would be at the performance, and I was afraid for it. It was just as if it were an ordinary person who was capable of dying. I nearly ran into the audience to look for the voice among the killed and wounded. But then I knew that if the voice was safe it would be in my dressing room. I rushed there and locked the door. I begged the voice, if it was still alive, to show itself to me. The voice did not reply, but then I heard a long beautiful wail. It was the song of Lazarus when, after hearing the Redeemer's voice, he wakes and sees the light of day. It was what we heard at Perros. And the voice sang, 'Come! And believe in me! Whosoever believes in me shall live! Walk! Whosoever believes in me shall never die!' The voice seemed to command me to believe in it and follow it. I did. I believed it. . . . I followed it and—this was the incredible thing—my dressing room seemed to lengthen out. Evidently it was an effect from mirrors, because I had the mirror in front of me . . . and suddenly I was outside the room without knowing how I got there!

"I was in a dark passage, with just a faint red light glimmering at a far corner of the wall. I was frightened, and I cried out. My voice was the only sound, for the singing and the violin had stopped. Suddenly a hand, stone-cold and bony, grabbed my wrist and did not let go. An arm went around my waist. I struggled for a while and then gave up trying to get away. I was dragged toward the light, and I saw that I was held by a man wearing a large cloak and wearing a mask that hid his whole face. I stiffened and opened my mouth to scream. But a hand closed it, a hand that I felt on my lips and my skin, a hand that smelled of death. Then I fainted.

"When I opened my eyes, we were still in darkness. From just the light of a lantern I could see a bubbling well. I was lying on the floor with my head on the knee of the masked man. He was bathing my forehead, and his hands smelled of death. I pushed him away and asked, 'Where am I? Where is the voice?' He only sighed. Then the black shape lifted me up onto a white warm shape. A friendly whinny greeted me, and I murmured 'César!' The animal quivered and I knew it was the white horse from the *Prophète* which I had often fed with sugar. The horse had disappeared, and there had been a rumor in the theater that it had been stolen by the Opera ghost. I believed in the voice, but I had never believed in the ghost. Now I began to wonder. I called for the voice to help me, because I never imagined that the voice and the ghost were one and the same. You have heard about the Opera ghost, haven't you, Raoul?"

"Yes, of course, but tell me what happened once you were on the white horse of the *Prophète*."

"I just let myself go. The black shape held me up, and I made no attempt to escape. I felt a curious peace come over me. I think we were in a narrow circular gallery running all around the Opera, which is immense, underground. The cellars are five stories deep and large enough to hold an entire town. I was once down to the third level, but never lower. There are black demons down there, standing in front of

boilers. They have shovels and pitchforks, and they poke at the fires and stir up the flames. If you come too close, they scare you off by suddenly opening the red mouths of their furnaces. . . . Anyway, riding on César's back, I saw the black demons in the distance again and again. At last they disappeared. The black shape was still holding me up, and César went on his own, sure-footed. We seemed to turn and turn and often went down a spiral stair into the very heart of the earth. Finally César raised his head, sniffed the air, and quickened his pace a little. Then he stopped. The darkness had lifted, and there was dampness in the air. A bluish light surrounded us. We were at the edge of a lake. The lead-colored water stretched into the distance and darkness, but the blue light illuminated the shore. I saw a little boat tied to an iron ring on the wharf!"

"A boat!"

"I knew that the lake and the boat really existed. But think of the conditions under which I got there! Anyhow, when the man's shape lifted me into the boat, my terror began again. The man sent César back, and I heard his hoofs receding while the man jumped into the boat. He rowed with a quick, powerful stroke. His eyes never left me. When we touched shore, the man lifted me again, and I cried out. Suddenly, I was silenced, dazed, by a dazzling light. I was put down in the middle of it. I was in a drawing room that seemed to be decorated with nothing but flowers. Magnificent flowers and ridiculous ones, some tied to silly baskets with silk ribbons, like those people send to dressing rooms on opening nights. In the middle of all the flowers stood the black-robed man, arms crossed. He said, 'Don't be afraid, Christine. You are in no danger.' *It was the voice!* I rushed at him and tried to tear off the mask, to see the face of the voice. He continued, 'You are in no danger, so long as you do not touch the mask.'

"He sat me in a chair, and he knelt before me and said nothing more. I realized that the voice, which I had recognized, was on its knees before me, *was a man*. A strange, terrible, eccentric man who had taken up living in the cellars of the Opera. And I began to cry. . . . The man must have read my thoughts, because he said, 'It is true, Christine! . . . I am not an angel, nor a ghost . . . I am Erik!' "

Christine's story was again interrupted. An echo seemed to repeat the name after her:

"Erik!"

Both Raoul and Christine turned around again, and they saw that night had fallen.

"Christine, something tells me that we are wrong to wait until tomorrow evening. We should leave at once!"

"If he does not hear me sing tomorrow, it will cause him great pain. He will certainly die when I leave him. But then it would count both ways . . . for we risk his killing us."

"Does he love you so much?"

"He would commit murder for me!"

"But we can find where he lives. We can go in search of him. Now that we know he is not a ghost, we can speak to him."

"No, no! There is nothing to be done except to run away!"

"But why, when you were able to get away from him, did you go back to him?

"You will understand that when I tell you how I got away."

"I hate him!" cried Raoul. "Christine, do you hate him, too?"

"No," Christine answered simply.

"No, of course not!" Raoul said angrily. "You love him! Your fear, then, is just love of a kind, the kind that gives you a thrill when you think of it. . . . Picture it: a man who lives in an underground palace!" Raoul gave a leer.

There was a terrible silence between the three of them—the two who spoke and the one who listened.

Finally Christine spoke:

"He fills me with horror. And yet I do not hate him. How can I hate him, Raoul? Think of Erik at my feet, in the house at the lake, underground. He accuses himself, curses himself, begs my forgiveness. He confesses his deceit. He loves me! He carried me off for love! He has imprisoned me for love! But he respects me. He crawls, moans, weeps. When I stood up and I told him that I would despise him if he did not let me go, he offered my freedom . . . to show me the mysterious road. . . . Only he stood up, too, and I was reminded that although he was not an angel, or a ghost, or a genius, he was the voice, for he sang. And I listened. . . and stayed. He sang me to sleep.

"In the morning I was alone, on a sofa in a simply furnished bedroom. The only exit was to a comfortable bathroom. I found a note in red ink, which said, 'My dear Christine, have no concern about your fate. You have no better nor more respectful friend in the world than myself. I am going out shopping now to get you all the things you need.' I was sure I had fallen into the hands of a madman. I became hysterical. I wanted to laugh and cry at the same time.

"That was my state of mind when he returned. He walked in through a door I had not seen before. His arms were full of packages and boxes that he carefully arranged on the bed as I heaped abuse on him. I told him to take off the mask if he was an honest man. He told me I would never see Erik's face. He also reproached me for not being dressed at two o'clock in the afternoon. He said a nice lunch was waiting in the dining room. Then he wound my watch and gave me thirty minutes to get ready.

"I was very angry. I slammed the door and went into the bathroom. When I came out, I felt better. Erik said that, even though he loved me, he would not say so unless I allowed him to. He promised that the rest of our time would be devoted to music. 'What do you mean by the rest of our time?' I asked. 'Five days,' he replied clearly. 'You will be free when the next five days are past. By that time you will have learned not to fear me. Then from time to time you will come to see your poor Erik!' He pointed to a small table with lunch. Erik did not eat or drink. I asked about his origins, and he said he had taken the name Erik by accident.

"After lunch he showed me around his apartment. His bedroom was like the room of a dead person. Everything was hung with black material. In the middle of the room was a canopy bed with red brocade hangings around an open coffin. 'This is where I sleep,' said Erik. The sight upset me so much I could not look at it.

"Then I saw the keyboard of an organ, and a music book filled with red notes. 'It is *Don Juan Triumphant*,' he said. 'I compose sometimes. I began that work twenty years ago. When I finish it, I will take it away in my coffin and never wake up again.' When I asked how often he worked at it, he explained, 'Sometimes I work on it day and night, two weeks at a time, living only on the music. And then I rest for years at a time.' When I asked him to play me something from his *Don Juan Triumphant*, he replied, 'You must never ask me that. My *Don Juan* burns, and yet he is not struck by fire from Heaven.' We returned to the drawing room. I noticed there were no mirrors in the whole apartment. I was about to comment on that when he sat down at the piano. 'There is, Christine, some music that consumes those who approach it. Fortunately you have not come to that yet. You would lose your pretty coloring and no one would know you when you returned to Paris. Let's sing something from the Opera, Christine Daaé!' He spoke the words as if they were an insult."

"What did you do?"

"I had no time to think about wht he meant. At once we began to sing the duet from *Otello*[2], and it was terrible. I sang Desdemona[3] with a terror I had never felt before. His voice thundered out his revenge in every note. Love, jealousy, hatred burst around us in terrible cries. Erik's mask was like the one of the Moor of Venice.[4] He *was* Otello. Suddenly, I had to see beneath the mask. With a movement I could not control, my fingers swiftly tore it away. Oh, horror, horror, horror!"

Christine stopped and thrice came the echoes of the night:

"Horror! . . . Horror! . . . Horror!"

Raoul and Christine held one another and raised their eyes to the skies. The stars shone in a clear and peaceful sky. Raoul said:

---

2. ***Otello***   opera by Giuseppi Verdi, based on Shakespeare's *Othello*
3. **Desdemona**   the female lead role in *Otello,* murdered by her husband, Othello, in a fit of jealousy
4. **Moor of Venice**   another name for the character Othello

"Strange, Christine, that the soft night is so full of plaintive sounds. One might think that it is sorrowing with us."

"When you know the secret, Raoul, your ears, like mine, will be full of sorrowful sounds." Christine took Raoul's hands in hers and, with a shiver, continued:

"If I live to be a hundred, I'll always remember the superhuman cry of grief and rage he uttered when the terrible sight appeared before my eyes. Raoul, you have seen death heads dried and withered with age. And you have seen Red Death stalking about at the last masked ball. But imagine Red Death's mask suddenly coming to life in order to express—through the four black holes of its eyes, nose, and mouth—the anger and fury of a demon! There was not a ray of light from the sockets. You can only see his blazing eyes in the dark!

"He hissed mad, incoherent words and curses at me. He leaned over me and screamed, 'Look! You wanted to see! See! Feast your eyes on my ugliness! Look at Erik's face! Now you know the face of the voice! You weren't content to hear me? You wanted to know what I looked like? Are you satisfied? I'm a very good-looking fellow, eh? When a woman has seen me, as you have, she belongs to me. She loves me forever. I am a kind of Don Juan, you know!' Drawing himself up to his full height, and wagging that hideous thing on his shoulders, he roared: 'Look at me! *I am Don Juan triumphant!*' I begged for mercy. When I turned my head away, he twisted his dead fingers into my hair and turned it back to him brutally."

"Enough! Enough!" cried Raoul. "I will kill him! Tell me how to find the dining room on the lake, Christine. I must kill him!"

"Be quiet, Raoul, if you want to know!"

"I want to know how and why you went back to him. I must know! But, in any case, I must kill him!"

"Oh, Raoul, listen! He dragged my by my hair, and then he hissed at me. 'Ah, I do frighten you, do I? Perhaps you think this head is just another mask? Well,' he roared, 'try it. Tear it off! You know how! Your hands! Give me your hands!' And he took my hands and dug them into his face. He tore his flesh with my nails, tore his terrible dead flesh with my nails! 'Know me!' he shouted, while his throat throbbed and panted like a furnace. 'Know that I am built up of death from head to foot! Know that it is a corpse that loves you and adores you and will never, never leave you! And you can never leave me! As long as you thought me handsome, you could come back. But now that you know my hideousness, you would run away for good. So I must keep you here! . . . Oh, Christine, why did you want to see me? My own father never saw me! And my mother, in order not to see me, gave me my first tiny mask!'

"He let go of me at last, and he dragged himself across the floor. He crawled away into his room, sobbing terribly, and closed the door. Soon I heard the organ. His *Don Juan Triumphant* was like nothing I had ever heard before. First it seemed like a long, awful, magnificent sob. Then it seemed to express every emotion, every sorrow mankind is capable of. I opened the door. Erik rose, but dared not turn in my direction. 'Erik,' I cried, 'show me your face without fear! I swear you are the most unhappy and the most magnificent of men. If ever again I shiver when I look at you, it will be because I am thinking of the greatness of your genius!' Erik turned. He believed me. And I believed myself. He fell at my feet with words of love. He kissed the hem of my dress and did not see me close my eyes.

"Now you know the tragedy. It went on for a fortnight. For a fortnight I lied to him. And the lies were as hideous as the monster who inspired them. But the lies were the price of my freedom. I burned his mask. He was like a dog with his master and paid me endless little attentions. Gradually I gave him enough confidence that he took me for walks along the banks of the river. He took me for rides in the boat. Toward the end, he took me through the gates that closed the underground passages at the Rue Scribe[5] in order to take me outside. We went for carriage rides in the Bois.[6] The night we met you was nearly fatal. He is so jealous of you! I told him you were going away soon. After a fortnight of horrible captivity, he believed me when I said, '*I will come back!*'"

"And you went back, Christine," groaned Raoul. "You had only gained your freedom for a few hours when you returned to Erik. Don't you remember the masked ball?"

"And don't you remember the great danger for us during those hours, Raoul? Each of my visits outside increased my horror of him. And each one, instead of calming him, made him mad with love. I am so frightened, so frightened . . ."

Raoul kissed her lips, but the night had grown dark and seemed no longer soft and calm. Their eyes were filled with the dread of Erik. And they saw, before they disappeared inside, high up above them, an immense black bird. It stared at them with blazing eyes from its perch on the string of Apollo's lyre.

---

5. **Rue** French word for *street* (Scribe is the name of the street near the Opera)
6. **Bois** short for the Bois de Boulogne, a wooded park in Paris

13 A Master Stroke

Raoul and Christine ran to escape from the roof and the blazing eyes that glowed in the dark. They stopped only when they reached the eighth floor. Suddenly a strange form stood before them and blocked the passage way.

"No, not this way!"

The form pointed to another passage to the wings of the theater. It wore a long frock-coat[1] and a pointed cap. Raoul wanted to ask some questions, but the form said:

"Quick! Go away quickly!"

And Christine was already dragging Raoul, making him run again.

"That's the Persian," Christine explained.

"What is he doing here?" asked Raoul.

"Nobody knows," Christine said as they went down one more floor. "He is always at the Opera."

"Christine, I am certain it would be better for us to go at once. Why wait for tomorrow? He may have heard us tonight."

"No, he is busy, I tell you. He is working on his music, and he is not thinking of us. Come to my dressing room."

"Shouldn't we meet outside the Opera?"

"Not until we leave for good. I have to keep my word or we'll have bad luck. I promised him I would

---

1. **frock-coat** knee-length man's coat, usually double-breasted with a skirt-like section in the front and back

see you only here. He knows all about our engage-
ment. He said, 'I trust you, Christine. M. Raoul de
Chagny is in love with you. Before he goes, I want him
to be as unhappy as I am!'"

"And are you still resolved to run away from
him?"

"Yes, tomorrow."

"Then I will be here at midnight tomorrow night.
I'll keep my promise, whatever happens. You say that,
after your performance, he will be waiting for you in
the dining room at the lake?"

"Yes."

"How can you reach the place?"

Christine opened a box and took out an enormous
key. "This," she explained, "is the key to the gate of
the underground passage in the Rue Scribe."

"It leads straight to the lake, doesn't it? Give it to
me, Christine."

"Never!" she said. "That would be treacherous!"

Suddenly Christine changed color. A deathly paleness spread across her features.

"Oh, Heaven! Oh, Heaven! Erik, have pity on
me!"

"What is it?" Raoul implored.

"The ring . . . the gold ring he gave me. When he
gave it to me, he said, 'I give you back your liberty so
long as you wear the ring. As long as you keep it, you
will be protected against danger and Erik remains
your friend. But woe to you if you lose it, for Erik will
have his revenge!' My dear, . . . my dear, the ring is
gone! . . . Woe to us both!"

They both looked for the ring, but could not find it.
Christine finally left him, wringing her hands and
rubbing her fingers, as if she hoped to bring the ring
back that way.

Raoul went home, greatly upset at all he had seen and heard.

"If I don't save her from the hands of that monster," he said aloud as he went to bed, "she will be lost. But I *will* save her!"

He put out the lamp and cursed Erik in the dark. Suddenly he sat up. Two eyes, like blazing coals, had appeared at the foot of his bed. They stared at him fixedly, cruelly, in the darkness. Raoul was no coward, but he trembled. He put out a groping hand toward the bedside table. He found and lit a match and candle. The eyes disappeared.

Raoul remembered what Christine had said about the eyes only showing in the dark. He rose, and looked around the room. He looked under the bed, like a child. Thinking himself to be absurd, he went the bed again and blew out the candles. Instantly, the eyes reappeared. He jumped up and ran to a chest of drawers and groped for his revolver. He got back into bed and put the revolver on the table beside his bed.

The eyes were still there at the foot of the bed. Were they inside the room, or behind the window on the balcony? That was what Raoul wanted to know. He also wanted to know if those eyes belonged to a human being.

Patiently, calmly, he picked up the revolver and took aim. He aimed a little above the two eyes. If these were eyes, then there would be a forehead above. If Raoul was not too clumsy . . .

The shot made a terrible noise in the dark. Footsteps came hurrying along the corridors. Raoul prepared to fire again. But this time, the two eyes were gone. Servants appeared carrying lights, and Count Philippe, very anxious:

"Raoul! Are you all right? For God's sake, what happened?"

"No, no, I'm all right. We shall see . . . "

He got out of bed, put on a robe and slippers, and took a lamp from one of the servants. He opened the window and stepped out on the balcony. All the while, the count was shaking him as if he were trying to awaken a sleepwalker.

"Raoul, Raoul, Raoul!"

The window had been pierced by a bullet at about a man's height. A trail of blood followed the balcony rail till it reached a gutter-spout. Then the marks went up the spout.

"My dear brother," said Count Philippe, "you have shot a cat."

"That's the thing," said Raoul with a grin. "That is quite possible. With Erik, you never know. Is it Erik? Is it a cat? Is it the ghost? No, with Erik, you can't tell!"

Raoul went on with these strange remarks, seemingly preoccupied with something outlandish. It seemed to the count that his mind had become unhinged. Later on, the examining magistrate, on receiving the police report, reached the same conclusion.

"Who is Erik?" asked the count.

"He is my rival. And if he's not dead, it's a pity!"

He dismissed the servants, and the two brothers were alone. Not out of earshot, the count's valet heard Raoul say distinctly and emphatically:

"I will carry off Christine Daaé tonight!"

This phrase was repeated afterward to M. Faure, the examining magistrate. No one ever knew exactly what else was said between the two brothers that night. The servants said that this was not their first quarrel. Their voices did carry through the walls, and the name Christine Daaé was heard several times.

In the morning the count took his breakfast in the study. He sent for Raoul, who arrived silent and gloomy. Philippe handed his brother a copy of the newspaper and said:

"Read this!"

The latest news is that there is a promise of love between Mlle. Christine Daaé, the opera singer, and M. le Vicomte Raoul de Chagny. According to the gossips, Count Philippe has sworn that this is *one* promise the de Chagnys will *not* keep. But we wonder how Count Philippe intends to prevent his brother from leading the new Marguerite to the altar. The two brothers are said to be very close, but we would not bet on brotherly love winning out over love pure and simple.

"You see, Raoul," said the count, "you are making us ridiculous! That girl has turned your head with her ghost stories!"

"Goodbye, Philippe."

"You are determined? You are going tonight? With her?"

No reply.

"Surely you wouldn't do anything so foolish? *I know how to prevent you!*"

"Goodbye, Philippe," said the viscount again, and he left the room.

Raoul spent the whole day preparing for the trip. He selected the horses, the carriage, the coachman, the provisions, the luggage, the money required, the route to be taken. All this was taken care of, and it occupied him until nine o'clock at night.

At nine o'clock, a traveling barouche[2] with its windows closed, took its place outside the Opera. It was drawn by two powerful horses and driven by a coachman whose face was almost hidden by the folds of a long muffler. In front of this carriage were three others. The first belonged to Carlotta, who had suddenly returned to Paris. The second was Sorelli's, and the third was that of Count Philippe de Chagny.

A shadow in a long black cloak and a soft felt hat walked along the sidewalk between the Opera and the carriages. The figure examined the barouche carefully, approached the horses and the coachman, then moved away without a word. The magistrate afterwards believed the person was the Vicomte Raoul de Chagny. I do not agree, seeing that the viscount was wearing a tall hat, which was later found. I am more inclined to think that the shadow was that of the ghost, who knew all about the plans, as the reader will soon see.

They were performing *Faust* before a large audience. The newspaper piece had had its effect: all eyes were on the box where Count Philippe sat alone. The women in the audience whispered about Raoul's absence, and they gave Christine Daaé a rather cool reception. They could not forgive her for aiming at so high a prize.

Christine was aware of the sentiment, and it puzzled her. Some in the audience made a point of turning toward the count when she sang:

> *I wish I could but know who was he*
> *That addressed me,*
> *If he was noble, or, at least, what his name is.*

---

2. **barouche** four-wheeled carriage with a high driver's seat in front and two double seats inside facing one another

Philippe seemed to pay no attention. His eyes were on the stage, but his thoughts seemed far away.

Christine began to lose her self-confidence. She trembled. Carolus Fonta wondered if she was ill, if she could keep going until the end of the act.

Just then Carlotta made her entrance in a box facing the stage: a sensational entrance. Christine saw her rival, and she thought she saw a sneer on Carlotta's lips. That saved her. She forgot everything in a desire to triumph once more. She sang with all her heart and soul. In the last act, when she began the call to the angels, everyone in the audience felt as though they, too, had wings.

In the center of the amphitheater, a man stood and remained standing, facing the singer. It was Raoul.

Holy angel, in Heaven blessed . . .

And Christine, arms outstretched, sang:

My spirit longs with thee to rest!

At that moment, the stage was plunged into darkness. It happened so quickly that the audience barely had time to gasp before the lights came back on. But Christine Daaé was gone!

Men rushed from the wings to the spot where Christine had been standing. Where had she gone? What witchcraft had snatched her away before thousands of onlookers, and from the arms of Carolus Fonta?

Raoul let out a cry. Count Philippe had leaped to his feet. People looked from the stage, to Raoul, to Philippe and wondered if the morning paper's paragraph had anything to do with this curious event.

Raoul hurriedly left the audience. The count disappeared from his box. While the curtain lowered, the regular patrons rushed for backstage. The rest of the audience waited.

At last, the curtain rose slowly, and Carolus Fonta stepped up to the conductor's platform. In a serious and sad voice he announced:

"Ladies and gentlemen, a very strange thing has occurred, and we are alarmed. Our sister-artist, Christine Daaé, has disappeared before our very eyes, and nobody can tell us how!"

14 *The Safety Pin*

Backstage it was chaos. Artists, scene changers, dancers, singers, patrons all were asking questions.

"What has become of her?"

"She's run away!"

"With the Vicomte de Chagny."

"No, with the count!"

"Here's Carlotta! Carlotta did the trick!"

"No, it was the ghost!"

In a corner, away from the noisy throng, three men stood talking and gesturing wildly. They were Gabriel, the chorus master, Mercier, the acting-manager, and Rémy, the secretary.

"I knocked at the door," said Rémy. "They didn't answer. Perhaps they aren't in the office. In any case we can't find out. They took the keys with them."

They meant the managers, who had given orders that they were not to be disturbed for any reason whatsoever.

"Even so," complained Gabriel, "a singer doesn't disappear every day!"

"I'll try again," said Rémy, and he disappeared.

At that moment the stage manager arrived.

"I've been down to the organ, and no one's there. I thought there might be someone at the organ who could tell us how the stage got to be suddenly dark. But Mauclair is nowhere to be found. What do you think of that?"

Mauclair was the gas man who created day or night time on the stage of the Opera.

"Mauclair gone?" repeated Mercier. "What about his assistants?"

"No Mauclair and no assistants! No one at the lights! I tell you that little girl did not run off by herself."

No one was to disturb the managers, on any account. Rémy had violated the order and had gotten nowhere. At that moment he returned from his second attempt with a curiously startled look on his face.

"Well, have you seen them?" asked Mercier.

"Moncharmin opened the door finally," Rémy said. "His eyes were bulging out of his head. I couldn't get a word in before he shouted, 'Have you got a safety pin? No? Well, then, clear out!' I tried to tell him what had happened on the stage, but he roared, 'A safety pin! Give me a safety pin at once!' A boy heard him—he was bellowing like a bull. He ran up and gave it to him. Then Moncharmin slammed the door in my face. I tell you, he was foaming at the mouth. This is all very unnatural. I'm not used to being treated like this."

Mercier muttered, "If people had listened to me, the police would have known everything long ago!" And he left to see what was going on at the managers' office.

"What's everything?" asked Rémy. "What should we have told the police, Gabriel? Aha, so you know something! Well you had better tell me or I'll shout out that you are all going mad! This evening our managers behaved like lunatics between the acts. Everyone was pointing at them."

"But what were the managers doing?" asked Gabriel, with a very innocent look.

"You saw them, you and Mercier! And you were the only two who did not laugh!"

"I don't understand," Gabriel said.

"What is this new mania of theirs? *Why won't they let anyone come near them?*"

"What?" asked Gabriel innocently. "*They won't let anyone come near them?*"

"*And they won't let anyone touch them!*"

"Really? *They won't let anyone touch them?* That is odd!"

"Good, you finally admit it, then! *And you know that they walk backwards!*"

"*Backwards?* You have seen our managers walk backwards? I thought only crabs walked backwards!"

"Don't laugh, Gabriel. Don't laugh."

"I'm not laughing," protested Gabriel, as serious as a judge.

"Perhaps you can explain this to me, then, Gabriel. When I went up to M. Richard in the foyer with my hand out, M. Moncharmin whispered to me, 'Go away! Go away! Whatever you do, don't touch M. Richard!' Do I have a disease?"

"That's incredible!"

"And later, I saw M. Richard turned around, bowed over *as if there was nobody in front of him, walking backwards.* And Moncharmin, behind Richard was also turned around and *walking backwards.* They went like that to the staircase leading up to their office. Now if that is not crazy, what is?"

"Perhaps they were practising a figure in the ballet," suggested Gabriel without much conviction.

The secretary Rémy was not amused at the joke, and he whispered in Gabriel's ear:

"Don't be so clever, Gabriel. Some of tonight's events are the responsibility of you and Mercier."

"What do you mean?" asked Gabriel.

"Christine Daaé is not the only one who disappeared

tonight. A short time ago, when Mother Giry came into the foyer, Mercier grabbed her by the hand and took her away."

"Really?" said Gabriel. "I did not see that."

"Yes, you did, Gabriel. You were with Mercier when he took her away. And since then you two have been seen, but Mother Giry has not!"

"What do you think we did with her?"

"You've locked her in Mercier's office, and anyone passing can hear her shouting."

At this point, Mercier returned out of breath.

"It's worse than I thought." he said in a gloomy voice. "I shouted for them to open the door, and Moncharmin did. He was very pale. I said, 'Someone has run off with Christine Daaé.' And what do you think he said? 'And a good job, too!' And he put this in my hand and shut the door."

Mercier opened his hand. Gabriel and Rémy looked. In his palm lay a safety pin.

"Strange! Strange!" muttered Gabriel. And he could not prevent a shiver.

At that moment a voice made all three jump.

"I beg your pardon, gentlemen. Could you tell me where is Christine Daaé?"

The question was so absurd that the men would have all roared with laughter, except that the look of sorrow on the newcomer's face filled them with pity. It was the Vicomte Raoul de Chagny.

15 *"Christine! Christine!"*

Raoul's first thought was to accuse Erik. And he rushed onto the stage in a fit of love and despair.

"Christine! Christine!" he called, as he felt she was calling him from the dark pit to which she had been taken. He wandered around the stage like a madman.

"Christine! Christine! . . ."

Hideous thoughts filled his brain. Erik must have discovered their secret. He must have known that Christine was deceiving him. What a vengeance he would take! Raoul ran to Christine's dressing room.

"Christine! Christine! . . . Why don't you answer? . . . Are you alive? . . ."

Scattered over the furniture were the clothes that his beautiful bride was to have worn at the hour of their flight. Why, oh why had she refused to leave earlier? Why as a last gesture of pity had she insisted on singing:

Holy angel, in Heaven blessed,
My spirit longs with thee to rest!

Suddenly he remembered something about a gate and the Rue Scribe. Christine had told him about an underground passage leading straight to the lake. The key was gone from the box, but he nevertheless ran to the Rue Scribe.

There, in the street, he felt the stones . . . felt for outlets . . . found iron bars . . . These? . . . Could these be air holes? . . . How dark it was through the bars! . . .

110

He listened. . . . Only silence . . . Around the building he came to bigger bars, immense gates! . . . It was the entrance to the Cour de l'Administration.[1]

Raoul rushed to the doorkeeper's home and inquired about the gate and the lake and the Rue Scribe. The woman answered:

"Yes, sir, I know there is a lake under the Opera. But I don't know which door leads to it. I've never been there!"

The woman screamed with laughter! In a rage, Raoul darted away, ran upstairs four at a time, through the business section of the Opera, and down once more to the lights of the stage. Suppose Christine had been found! He stopped a group of men and asked:

"I beg your pardon, gentlemen. Could you tell me where Christine Daaé is?"

Somebody laughed.

At the same moment another crowd of men entered. There was one man at the center who seemed quite calm and had a very pleasant face, curly hair, and serene blue eyes. Mercier, the acting-manager pointed him out, saying:

"This is the gentleman to whom you should put your question, monsieur. Let me introduce you to M. Mifroid, the police commissioner."

"Ah, M. le Vicomte de Chagny! Delighted to meet you. Would you mind coming with me? Let's go to the managers' office and let them in on what's going on here!"

Amidst the confusion as the men left the stage, Mercier slipped a key into Gabriel's hand:

---

1. **Cour de l'Administration** business side, including business offices, of the Opera House.

"This is going very badly," he whispered. "You had better let Mother Giry out."

Gabriel moved away.

The managers' door was still closed. Mercier pounded in vain.

"Open in the name of the law!" commanded M. Mifroid in a loud and rather anxious voice.

At last the door opened, and the crowd poured in. Raoul was the last to enter. As he was about to go into the room, he felt a hand on his shoulder and these words in his ear:

"Erik's secrets concern no one but himself!"

Raoul turned and saw that the hand was now held up to the lips of a person he had seen once before. With his ebony skin, jade eyes, and astrakhan[2] cap, it was the Persian.

The stranger put his finger to his lips again, signalling silence. As Raoul was about to ask the reason for his involvement, he bowed and disappeared.

---

2. astrakhan cap hat made of wool with a curly, looped pile

16 *Mme. Giry and the Ghost*

We will follow the commissioner into the managers' office. But first, my duty as an historian requires me to describe some events that were taking place in that office while Rémy and Mercier tried in vain to enter.

The ghost had calmly been paid his first allowance of 20,000 francs. It happened this way. One morning the managers found a note from O.G., which included an envelope marked "Monsieur O.G. (Private)." The note directed them to put twenty notes of a thousand francs each into the enclosed envelope, seal it with their own seal, and hand it to Mme. Giry, who would do what was necessary.

The managers told the whole story to Gabriel and Mercier, swearing them to secrecy. Then they put the money in the envelope and gave it to Mme. Giry, who showed no surprise. While the men watched from a hiding place, she went straight to Box 5 and placed the envelope on the little shelf attached to the ledge.

Nobody touched the envelope during the performance or after. Tired of waiting, the men opened the envelope, on which the seals had not been broken.

At first glance it appeared that the money was still there, but a closer examination revealed that the real bills had been replaced by play money!

The managers were furious! Richard said:

"Old O. G. has won the first round, but we will win the second."

He was referring to the next month's allowance.

114

In spite of their words, the managers had been so soundly tricked that they suffered some dejection. Now they had to wait a month before taking action. In the meantime, they kept an eye on Mother Giry, in spite of the fact that Richard still considered her an idiot.

The next payment fell on the same day that Christine Daaé disappeared. A morning note from the ghost reminded the managers that the money was due:

> Do just as last time. It went very well.
> Put the 20 thousand-franc notes in an envelope and hand it to the excellent Mme. Giry.

The note was accompanied by the usual return envelope. They had only to insert the money. They did this about a half hour before the curtain rose on the first act of *Faust*. Richard showed the envelope to Moncharmin. Then he inserted the twenty thousand-franc notes into the envelope without closing it.

"Now," he said, "let's have Mother Giry here."

The woman entered with a sweeping curtsy. She still wore her old black taffeta dress and dingy bonnet. She was in a good mood:

"Good evening, gentlemen! It's time for the envelope, I suppose?"

"Yes, Mme. Giry," said Richard amiably, "for the envelope and something else besides."

"At your service, M. Richard, and what is the something else, please?"

"First, Mme. Giry, a little question."

"By all means, M. Richard. Mme. Giry is here to serve you."

"Ah, how delightful . . . here it is. We shall soon understand one another. The story of the ghost is all humbug, isn't it? Just between ourselves . . . it has lasted long enough."

Mme. Giry looked at the managers as if they had spoken Chinese.

"I don't understand. What do you mean?"

"You understand quite well. In any case, you will have to understand. . . . First of all, tell us his name."

"Whose name?"

"The name of the man whose accomplice you are."

"The ghost's accomplice? I? In what, pray?"

"You do what he wants."

"Oh! . . . He's not troublesome, you know."

"How much does he give you for bringing the envelope?"

"Ten francs, but that's not the point, sirs."

"Indeed?" sneered Richard. "Tell me why you have given your devotion to this ghost for just a few francs!"

"It's like this . . . only he doesn't like me to talk about his business. . . . Well, it was in Box 5 one evening that I found a letter to me written in red ink. I know it by heart. I'll never forget it if I live to be a hundred!"

Madame Giry recited the letter with eloquence.

Madame:

1825. Mme. Ménétrier, leader of the ballet, became Marquise de Cussy.

1832. Mlle. Marie Taglioni, dancer, became Comtesse Gilbert des Voisins.

1846. La Sota, dancer, married a brother of the King of Spain.

1847. Lola Montez, dancer, became the wife of Louis of Bavaria and was created Countess of Landsfeld.

1848. Mlle. Maria, dancer, became Baronne d'Herneville.

Richard and Moncharmin listened as the woman went on and on with her list of marriages. At last, in a voice bursting with pride:

1885. Meg Giry, Empress!

"Gentlemen, I had heard a lot about the ghost, but only half believed in him. But the day that he declared my little Meg—the flesh of my flesh, fruit of my womb—would be empress, I believed altogether."

"You have never seen him. He only speaks to you. Yet you believe all he says?"

"I owe it to him that my little Meg was promoted to leader of a row. I said, 'If my little Meg is going to be empress in 1885, she had better become a leader at once.' So the ghost just had a word with M. Poligny and the thing was done."

"So you saw him with M. Poligny?"

"No more than anyone. But I think there were always secrets between the ghost and M. Poligny. Anything the ghost wanted, M. Poligny did. He refused the ghost nothing."

Richard interrupted:

"I don't care about M. Poligny. I care only about Mme. Giry. Madame, do you know what is in this envelope?"

"Of course not," she said.

"Well, look!"

"Thousand-franc notes!" she cried.

"Yes, Mme. Giry, thousand-franc notes, and you knew it! . . . And now I will tell you the second reason why I sent for you. Mme. Giry, I am going to have you arrested, as a thief!"

Mme. Giry moved quickly. She gave M. Manager Richard a mighty box on the ear, before M. Manager

Moncharmin could intervene. But it was not her hand that struck the blow, but the envelope. It opened with the impact, scattering bank notes like a giant whirl of butterflies.

The managers shouted, and they both fell to their knees. They feverishly picked up the precious scraps of paper. Above their heads, Mme. Giry's three teeth were clashing noisily:

"I, a thief! . . . "I, a thief! . . . I?"

She choked with rage. She shouted:

"I never heard of such a thing!"

And she advanced on M. Richard:

"You ought to know better than I where the 20,000 francs went!"

"I?" asked Richard astonished. "And how should I know?"

He felt himself turning red under Moncharmin's eyes. He took Mme. Giry's wrist and shook it violently. In a voice that growled and rolled like thunder, he roared:

"Why should I know better than you where the money went to? Why? Answer me!"

"Because it went into your pocket!"

Richard would have rushed Mme. Giry if his partner had not restrained him. And Moncharmin asked her, more gently, to explain.

"I never said M. Richard put the money in his pocket himself. I never said that, seeing that it was myself that put it there. There! It's out! . . . May the ghost forgive me!"

Mme. Giry, like the martyr she was, raised her head. Her face beamed with her own innocence.

"You tell me there were twenty thousand-franc notes that I put into M. Richard's pocket. I tell you I did not know that. Neither did M. Richard, for that matter."

"Aha!" said Richard, assuming a swaggering air which Moncharmin did not like. "I knew nothing either! You put 20,000 francs in my pocket and I knew nothing either! I am very glad to hear that, Mme. Giry!"

"Yes," said the woman, "it's true. We neither of us knew anything. But you, you must have found out!"

Richard would certainly have swallowed Mme. Giry alive if Moncharmin had not protected her. He continued the questioning:

"What envelope did you put in M. Richard's pocket? It was not the one we watched you take to Box 5. And yet you say it was the one with 20,000 francs in it."

"I beg your pardon," explained Mme. Giry. The envelope you gave me was the one I slipped into M. Richard's pocket. The envelope I took to Box 5 was another one. The ghost had given it to me beforehand, and I had hid it up my sleeve."

Saying that, the woman took from her sleeve another similar envelope, ready prepared and similarly addressed. The managers took it from her and examined it. It was filled and fastened with their own seals. They opened it to discover another quantity of play money.

"How simple!" said Richard.

"How simple," repeated Moncharmin. He stared at Mme. Giry.

"So it was the ghost who gave you this envelope and told you to substitute it? And it was the ghost who told you to put the original in M. Richard's pocket?"

"Yes, it was the ghost."

"Then would you mind showing us how you did it?" asked Moncharmin. He kept one eye on Richard, and one eye on Mme. Giry. The effort was likely to strain his sight, but Moncharmin was prepared to go to any length to discover the truth.

Mme. Giry took the envelope with the twenty notes inside and headed for the door.

"Oh, no! Oh, no! We're not going to be tricked a second time. Once bitten, twice shy! Just *tell* us how you did it!"

"I slip it in your pocket when you least expect it. You know I am always around the stage and the balconies, and the dressing rooms. I come and go as I please. So do you, sir. There are lots of people around. I just pass behind you and slip the envelope into your coat-tail pocket."

"That's a lie! I spent that evening watching Box 5 and the sham envelope you put there. I didn't go to the foyer for a second."

"No, sir, and I did not give you the envelope that evening. It was at the next performance, when the undersecretary of state. . . ."

M. Richard suddenly interrupted Mme. Giry:

"That's true. I remember now! The undersecretary went behind the scenes. He and his chief clerk were in the foyer itself . . . I suddenly turned around . . . you had passed behind me . . . You seemed to push me . . . Oh, I can see it still!"

"That's it, sir. I had just finished my little business. That coat-tail pocket was very handy!"

"It's very clever of O. G. No intermediary between the man who gives the 20,000 and the man who receives it. He could come and get the money when he wanted to. He had only to take it from my pocket, since I myself didn't know it was there. It's wonderful!"

"Oh, wonderful!" Moncharmin agreed. "But you forget that I provided 10,000 francs of the 20. And nobody put anything in my pocket!"

17 *The Safety Pin Again*

We now come to the strange behaviors observed by M. Rémy. It was arranged by Richard and Moncharmin that Richard should repeat the exact movements he made on the night the first 20,000 francs disappeared. It was Moncharmin's responsibility not to lose sight of Richard's coat-tail pocket, into which Mme. Giry was to slip the francs.

M. Richard stood on the spot where he had been with the undersecretary. M. Moncharmin took up his position to watch. Mme. Giry passed by, rubbed against Richard, got rid of the francs in his pocket, and disappeared. . . . Or rather she was whisked away. In accordance with instructions given by Moncharmin, Mercier took the good lady to his office and locked her in. This was done in order to make it impossible for her to contact the ghost.

Meanwhile M. Richard walked bending and bowing, just as if the undersecretary were really in front of him. And when people approached the manager, Moncharmin pushed them away and ordered them "not to touch *M. le directeur*." They went about like this for some time. No one had brushed up against Richard since Mme. Giry had. Again, this unusual method of walking attracted a good deal of attention, but the managers themselves gave thought only to their 20,000 francs.

They were now at the passage leading to the offices of the management. In this way, Moncharmin could see anyone approaching from the back. Richard himself could see anyone from the front. As they reached the passageway, Richard said in a low voice:

"I am sure no one has touched me. Drop back a distance now, and watch me until I come to the door of the office. It is better not to arouse suspicion, and we can see anything that happens."

"No, Richard! You walk ahead and I'll walk immediately behind you. I won't leave you by a step!"

"In that case," exclaimed Richard, "no one will ever steal our money!"

"I should hope not!" declared Moncharmin.

Two minutes later, the two managers were locked in their office.

"Last time," Moncharmin recalled, "we stayed locked up here until you left the Opera to go home."

"Yes," said Richard, "and no one came and disturbed us. So I must have been robbed on my way home."

"No," said Moncharmin, "because I took you home in my cab. The 20,000 francs disappeared at your place; there's not a shadow of a doubt!"

"Moncharmin, I've had enough of this! Do you dare suspect me?"

"Richard, I've had too much of it! Stop the joke!" said Moncharmin, taking up the newspaper to read.

Richard snatched the paper from his hands, and said:

"Look, if—like last time—I had spent the evening alone with you and you brought me home, and at the moment you were leaving I noticed that 20,000 francs were no longer in my pocket, they stood a very good chance of being in yours!"

Moncharmin leaped up. "Oh!" he shouted, "A safety pin!"

"Why?"

"To fasten you up with! A safety pin! A safety pin!"

"You want to fasten me up with a safety-pin?"

"Yes! Then no matter where—here, or on the drive home, or at your place—you will feel the hand that pulls at your pocket, and you will see it's not mine! You're suspecting me now? A safety pin!"

We know how, at this same moment, Rémy, who had no safety pin, was greeted by Moncharmin. We know that a boy produced the pin so eagerly sought. What happened next was that Moncharmin locked the door again. He checked the franc notes. They were still in Richard's pocket, and they were still genuine. He put them back in the pocket and pinned them carefully. And the two men waited for midnight.

"You know," said Richard, "suppose it were the ghost who puts the magic envelopes on the table . . . who talks in Box 5 . . . who killed Joseph Buquet . . . who unhooked the chandelier . . . and who robbed us! After all, there is no one here except you and me. And if the money disappears and neither of us has anything to do with it, then we will have to believe in the ghost."

The clock struck midnight. The two men gave a sigh and stood up.

"We can go home now," said Moncharmin.

"Agreed," said Richard.

"Before we go, do you mind if I look in your pocket?"

"Of course, Moncharmin, if you must. Well?" he asked as Moncharmin was feeling the pocket.

"I can feel the pin."

"As you said, we cannot be robbed without noticing it."

But Moncharmin, his hands still fumbling, bellowed:

"I can feel the pin, but I can't feel the notes!"

Richard tore off the coat. They turned the pocket inside out. *It was empty.* The curious thing was that the pin remained, stuck in the same place.

"The ghost!" muttered Moncharmin.

But Richard sprang upon his partner.

"No one but you has touched my pocket! Give back the money! Give back the 20,000 francs!"

"On my soul," gasped Moncharmin, who was about to faint, "on my soul, I haven't got it!"

Just then someone knocked at the door. Moncharmin answered it automatically, and seemed hardly to recognize Mercier, his business manager. He exchanged a few words without knowing what he was saying and, with an unconscious movement, put the safety pin into the hand of his bewildered employee.

18 *The Commissioner*

The first words the commissioner spoke on entering the managers' office were:

"Is Christine Daaé here?"

"Christine Daaé here?" echoed Richard. "No. Why?"

Moncharmin didn't have enough strength left to utter a word.

Richard repeated:

"Why do you ask if Christine Daaé is here, sir?"

"Because she has to be found," declared the commissioner of police solemnly.

"Found? Has she disappeared?"

"During the performance!"

"During the performance? Extraordinary!"

"Yes, it is. And what is also extraordinary is that you are first learning about it from me!"

In the face of this fresh trouble, Richard pulled a few hairs out of his mustache without knowing what he was doing.

"So she . . . she disappeared during the performance?" he repeated.

"Yes, as she was calling for the aid of the angels, she was carried off. I doubt, however, that it was an angel."

A young man, pale and trembling, offered an opinion to the contrary:

"Christine Daaé *was* carried off by an angel, and I can give you his name . . . when we are alone."

"Ah, M. le Vicomte de Chagny!" the police commissioner said. And he cleared the room except for Raoul and the managers.

Raoul spoke:

"*M. le commissaire*,[1] the angel is called Erik. He lives in the Opera and he is the Angel of Music!"

"This is curious!" M. Mifroid said. Turning to the managers, he asked, "Do you have an Angel of Music on the premises?"

The two managers shook their heads, without speaking.

"Oh," said the viscount, "those gentlemen have heard of the Opera ghost. Well, I know that the Opera ghost and the Angel of Music are the same person. His name is Erik."

"Gentlemen, do you know the Opera ghost?"

Richard stood up, with the remaining hairs from his mustache in his hand.

"No, M. Commissioner. No, we don't know him, but we wish we did. This very day he robbed us of 20,000 francs!"

And Richard gave a terrible look at Moncharmin. With the look, he threatened to tell the whole story if he did not get the money back.

Mifroid looked at the managers and Raoul by turns:

"A ghost," he said, "who on the same evening carries off a singer and steals 20,000 francs! He must be very busy. Let's take the questions in order. M. de Chagny, you believe that Mlle. Christine Daaé was carried off by an individual called Erik? Do you know this person? Have you seen him?"

"Yes, in a churchyard."

"Of course! . . . That's where ghosts often hang out . . ."

---

1. *M. le commissaire* French title for Mister Commissioner, the M. standing for *Monsieur*

"Sir," said Raoul, "I am in full possession of my senses. I would like to convince you of that as quickly as possible. Unfortunately I have to tell you the strangest story you will have ever heard from the very beginning, or you will never believe me. I will tell you all I know about the Opera ghost, which isn't much! . . ."

"Go on! Go on!" exclaimed Richard and Moncharmin, suddenly very interested.

Raoul began to tell his story of Perros, and death's heads and enchanted violins. His listeners soon decided that he had completely lost his mind. But they never had the chance to say so, because there was a knock on the door and a man entered.

The man was curiously dressed in an enormous frock-coat and a tall hat. He approached the commissioner and whispered in his ear. It was no doubt an important communication.

M. Mifroid never took his eyes off Raoul. At last, he said:

"Let's talk about you a little. You were going to carry off Mlle. Daaé tonight yourself, were you not?"

"Yes, *M. le commissaire.*"

"After the performance?"

"Yes, *M. le commissaire.*"

"All the arrangements were made?"

"Yes, *M. le commissaire.*"

"When you left your carriage outside the building, did you notice there were three other carriages there as well?"

"I didn't pay any attention to that."

"One of the carriages belongs to your brother, M. le Comte de Chagny."

"Very likely."

"Well, M. de Chagny, let me tell you that only one

carriage is gone. Your brother has been smarter than you. It is he who carried off Christine Daaé!"

"Impossible!"

"His carriage has been seen crossing and leaving Paris, by the Brussels road."

Raoul jumped up and rushed out of the office. But he was stopped at the very first corridor by a tall figure that blocked his way. He impatiently raised his eyes. He recognized the astrakhan cap and stopped:

"It's you!" he cried. "You who know Erik's secrets and don't want me to speak of them. Who are you?"

"You know who I am! . . . I am the Persian!"

19 The Viscount and the Persian

Raoul remembered that his brother had once showed him this mysterious person. Nothing was known about him, except that he lived in a small old-fashioned apartment on the Rue de Rivoli.

"Where are you going so fast, M. de Chagny?"

"Can't you guess? To Christine Daaé's assistance."

"Then, sir, stay here, because she is here!"

"With Erik?"

"I was at the performance and no one in the world but Erik could have pulled off such a kidnapping! Oh," he sighed, "I recognize the monster's touch! . . ."

"Sir," said Raoul, "I don't know what your intentions are. The commissioner of police tells me my brother, Count Philippe, has carried Christine off. You tell me she is here! I believe you, but what can you do to help me? That is, to help Christine Daaé?"

"I can try to take you to her . . . and to him," said the Persian.

"Let's not waste any more time, then. I place myself entirely in your hands. Why wouldn't I when you are the only one to believe me . . . the only one not to smile when Erik's name is mentioned!"

"Silence! Do not mention that name here. We need to say 'he' and 'him,' so there will be less danger of attracting his attention."

"So you think he is near?"

"It is quite possible, sir, if he is not with his victim *in the house at the lake.* If he is not there, he may be here, in this wall, in this floor, in the ceiling! . . . Come on!"

The Persian, warning Raoul to walk softly, led him down passages that Raoul had never seen before, even when Christine took him for walks through the corridors. They entered a deserted square, an immense space lit by a small lamp. Then they went up and down staircases and found themselves in front of a door the Persian opened with a key.

"Your hat will be in your way, sir," said the Persian. "You should leave it in the dressing room."

"What dressing room?" asked Raoul.

"Christine Daaé's."

The Persian led Raoul through a door he had just opened, and the actress's room was opposite. He pushed the young man in the room, which looked as Raoul had left it a short time earlier. Closing the door, the Persian went to a thin partition that separated the dressing room from the room next door. He listened then coughed loudly.

Soon there was a sound of someone stirring, then a finger tapped on the partition.

"Come in," said the Persian.

A man entered, also wearing an astrakhan cap and a long overcoat. He bowed, took a carved wooden case from under his coat, put it on the dressing-room table, bowed again, and went to the door.

"Well done, Darius. Let no one see you go out."

The man glanced down the corridor, then swiftly disappeared.

The Persian opened the case. Inside was a pair of long pistols.

"When Christine Daaé was carried off, I sent word to my servant to bring me these pistols. I have had them a long time, and they are reliable in a duel."

The Persian handed one to Raoul and said, "In the

duel we will fight, we shall be two to one. But you must be prepared for anything. We shall be fighting the most terrible adversary you can imagine. But you love Christine Daaé, don't you?"

"I worship the ground she walks on. But you, sir, you don't know her. You must certainly hate Erik!"

"No, sir," said the Persian sadly. "I don't hate him. If I did, he would have been stopped long ago."

"Has he done you harm?"

"I have forgiven him any harm he has done me."

The Persian got a stool and set it against the wall opposite the mirror. He climbed up and, with his nose to the wallpaper, seemed to look for something. Finally, he seemed satisfied and, raising his finger above his head, pressed a corner in the pattern of the paper. Then he turned around, jumped off the stool, walked to the mirror wall and felt the mirror.

"In half a minute," he said, "the mirror will turn on its pivot, and we will be *on his road*! Put down your hat, please . . . there . . . and now cover your shirt front as much as you can with your coat . . . as I am doing. . . . Bring the lapels together . . . turn up the collar. . . . We must make ourselves as invisible as possible."

"It's not moving," said Raoul impatiently.

"Be patient! We shall do all that is humanly possible to do! But he may stop us at the first step! He commands these walls, doors, and trapdoors. In my country, he was known as 'the trapdoor lover.' And he built these walls."

Raoul was about to ask a question, when the Persian made a sign for him to be quiet and pointed to the glass. Their reflections shivered, then all became stationary again.

"Look out!" said the Persian, "and be ready to fire."

He himself raised his pistol opposite the glass. Raoul imitated the movement. With his free arm, the Persian drew the young man to his chest. Suddenly the mirror turned. In a blinding daze of cross-lights, it turned like a revolving door, taking Raoul and the Persian with it and throwing them from full light into deep darkness.

20 In the Cellars of the Opera

"Keep your hand high, ready to fire!" repeated Raoul's companion quickly.

The wall closed again behind them, and the two men stood motionless, without breathing.

At last, the Persian made a move. Raoul heard him on his knees, feeling for something in the dark. He could not see the Persian, but he felt him by his side and heard him whisper:

"Follow me and do everything I do."

The Persian, still on his knees, opened a trapdoor, from which came a pale glow of light. Holding his pistol in his teeth, he hung by his hands from the rim of the opening and slid into the cellar below.

Strangely enough, Raoul had absolute confidence in the Persian, though he knew nothing about him. Besides, he had to reach Christine at all costs. He therefore went on his knees and hung from the trapdoor with both hands.

"Let go!" a voice said.

He dropped into the arms of the Persian, who told him to lie down flat, closed the trapdoor and crouched down beside him.

Raoul and the Persian were completely hidden behind a wooden partition. Near them, a small staircase led to a little room in which they could hear Commissioner Mifroid walking up and down, asking questions. The faint light was just enough for Raoul to distinguish shapes around him. Looking around, he could not restrain a dull cry;

there were three corpses there!

The first one lay on the narrow landing of the staircase. The other two had rolled to the bottom. If Raoul had reached his hand through the partition, he could have touched them.

"Silence!" whispered the Persian.

He, too, had seen the bodies and gave a one-word explanation:

"*He!*"

Just then the police commissioner tried to open the door to the little stairway. It resisted. The stage manager forced it with his shoulder. He saw, at the same time, that he was pushing a human body and let out an exclamation, for he recognized the body.

"Mauclair, the gas man. Poor devil! He is dead!"

But Commissioner Mifroid was stooping over the body.

"No, not dead," he said. "He is dead drunk, which is not quite the same thing."

"If so, it is the first time!" said the stage manager. "Perhaps someone gave him a narcotic. That is quite possible."

By the light of a little red lantern, they saw the other two bodies. The stage manager recognized Mauclair's assistants. Mifroid bent down and listened to their breathing.

"They are sound asleep," he said. "Very curious business! Someone interfered with the gas man and his staff. But what a strange idea to kidnap someone from off the stage! . . . Send for the theater doctor, please." And Mifroid repeated, "Curious, definitely curious!"

The stage manager said reluctantly, "This is not the first time Mauclair has fallen asleep in the theater. I remember finding him once snoring in his little area, his snuff box beside him."

"Was that long ago?" asked Mifroid.

"No, not very. . . Wait a minute! . . . It was the night that Carlotta—you know, sir—the night she gave her famous 'co-ack'!"

"So Mauclair takes snuff, does he?" M. Mifroid asked carelessly.

"Yes, sir . . . Look, there is his snuff box on that little shelf."

"So do I," said Mifroid and put the snuff box in his pocket."

Raoul and the Persian, unobserved, watched the three bodies being removed by a number of people who were followed by the Commissioner and all the people with him. When they were alone, the Persian made a sign for Raoul to stand up. Raoul did so, but the Persian had to remind him to keep his hand before his eyes.

"It tires the hand unnecessarily," said Raoul. "If I do fire, I can't be sure of my aim."

"Then shift the pistol to your other hand," said the Persian.

"I can't shoot with that hand."

Then the Persian made this strange reply:

"Actually, it's not a question of shooting with the right or the left. It's a question of holding one of your hands as though you were going to pull a trigger with your arm bent. As for the pistol itself, you can put it in your pocket. This is a matter of life and death. Now, silence and follow me!"

The Opera cellars are enormous and there are five of them. Raoul and the Persian descended to the third cellar. Their progress was still lit by a distant lamp. The lower they went, the more careful the Persian was. He kept on turning to Raoul to see if he was holding his arm properly.

Suddenly a loud voice made them stop. Someone above shouted:

"All door-shutters on the stage! All door-shutters! The police commissioner wants them!"

"Hang it!" muttered the Persian. "They might easily find us. . . . Let us get away quickly! . . . Your hand up, sir, ready to fire! . . . Bend your arm. . . more . . . that's it! . . . Hand at the level of your eye, as though you were fighting a duel. Quick! Downstairs! Level of your eye! . . . Question of life or death! . . . Here, this way, these stairs!" They reached the fifth cellar. "What a duel! What a duel, sir."

Once in the fifth cellar, the Persian drew a breath. He seemed more confident, but he never changed the position of his hand. Raoul remembered the Persian's words: "These pistols can be relied upon," and wondered why someone would be so gratified to depend on something that he didn't intend to use!

Something moved in the darkness in front of them.

"On your stomach!" whispered the Persian.

The two men lay on the floor.

They were just in time. A shade, this time carrying no light, passed. It passed close enough to touch. On its head was a soft felt hat. . . . It moved away, dragging its foot along the walls and sometimes kicking into a corner.

"Is that someone in the theater police?" Raoul asked.

"It's someone much worse!" replied the Persian.

"It's not *he*?"

"*He*? . . . If he comes in front of us, we can see his yellow eyes! That is more or less our safeguard tonight. But he may choose to come from behind, stealing up. Then we are dead men, unless we keep our hands as though we are about to fire. At the level of your eyes, in front!"

Suddenly a fantastic face came into sight . . . a whole fiery face, not just two yellow eyes!

Yes, a head of fire came toward them, at a man's height, but with no body attached.

"Oh!" said the Persian, "I've never seen this before! The fireman Pampin was right, after all. What is the flame? It is not *he*, but he may have sent it! Take care! Your hand at eye level, for Heaven's sake, at eye level! I know most of his tricks . . . but not this one! . . . Come on, run! . . . It is safer. Hand at the level of your eyes!"

After a few seconds they stopped. They turned their heads, and they again saw the head of fire behind them. It had followed them, and it must have run, too, and perhaps faster than they did. It seemed closer.

They continued their retreat, but the fiery face came on, came on, gaining on them. They could see its features clearly now. The eyes were round and staring, the nose a little crooked and the mouth large, with a drooping lower lip. It was very like the eyes, nose, and lips of the moon when it is quite red, bright red. But as the red moon approached there was a scraping, scratching, grating sound that came with it.

The Persian and Raoul could retreat no more and they flattened themselves against the wall. They didn't know what would happen next with the head of fire—especially now because of the intense swarming sound it made. The sound seemed made up of hundreds of little sounds that moved in the darkness under the fiery face.

The two companions felt their hair stand on end as the waves of noise came toward them. The little waves

passed between their legs, climbing up their legs, and Raoul and the Persian could not hold back their cries of horror and pain. Nor could they continue to hold their hands at the level of their eyes.

Their hands went down to their legs to push back the waves, which were filled with little legs and nails and claws and teeth.

"Don't move! Don't move! Whatever you do, don't come after me! . . . I am the rat catcher! . . . Let me pass with my rats! . . . "

And the head of fire disappeared. In order not to scare the rats in front of him, the rat catcher had turned the light on himself, lighting up his own head. Now, to hasten their flight, he lit the dark space in front of him. He jumped along, dragging with him the waves of scratching rats.

The two men breathed again, though still trembling.

"Are we far from the lake, sir?" asked Raoul. "When shall we get there? Take me to the lake. . . . When we are there, we will call out! . . . Christine will hear us! . . . And he will hear us, too! . . . And as you know him, we shall talk to him!"

The Persian tried to calm the young man.

"We have only one means of saving Christine Daaé, believe me. That is to enter the house unseen by the monster."

"And how can we enter the house on the lake without crossing the lake?"

"We need to go back to the third cellar, where we had to escape the shade. We will go there now. . . . I will tell you," said the Persian in a changed voice. "I will tell you the exact place. It is between a set piece and a discarded scene from *Roi de Lahore*, exactly where Joseph Buquet died. Follow me now. Hand at eye level."

The Persian went in front of Raoul. He sought his way through a cellar used particularly for the water-works, stopping once to avoid meeting some water-men. They passed men tending some kind of underground forge, and Raoul recognized the demons Christine had described seeing during her first captivity.

In this way, the two arrived beneath the huge cellars below the stage. They must have been at the bottom of the "tub" and very deep. (Remember that the earth was dug out fifty feet below the water that lay under that whole part of Paris.)

The Persian touched a wall and said:

"If I am not mistaken, this is a wall of the house on the lake."

Raoul listened eagerly, but he only heard distant steps on the floor of the upper portions of the theater.

"Look out! Keep your hand up! And silence. We shall try another way of getting in!"

And he led the way to the small staircase they had come down some time earlier. They went up, stopping at each step and listening, till they came up to the third cellar. Here the Persian motioned Raoul to crawl on both knees and one hand, keeping the other hand positioned as always.

They finally reached the end wall. The Persian felt it, then pressed against it, just as he had in Christine's dressing room. A stone gave way, leaving a hole. He made a sign for Raoul to do as he did. Cocking his pistol, and still on his knees, he wiggled into the hole in the wall. He stopped right away. Raoul heard him whisper:

"We shall have to drop a few yards, without noise. Take off your boots."

The Persian handed his own shoes to Raoul:

"Put them outside the wall. We'll pick them up when we leave."[1]

"I'm going to hang by my hands from the edge of the stone and let myself drop into the house. You must do exactly the same. Don't be nervous. I'll be below to catch you."

Raoul heard a dull sound, evidently the Persian's fall, then he dropped down. The two stood motionless, listening.

The darkness was thick around them, and the silence was heavy and terrible.

The Persian turned on the dark lantern again, looking for the hole through which they had come. Failing to find it, he said:

"The stone has closed by itself."

He then played the lamp over the wall and floor. He stooped to pick up something from the floor. It was a piece of cord which he examined for a second, then threw away with horror:

"The Punjab lasso!" he muttered.

"What is that?" Raoul asked.

The Persian shivered. "It might well be the rope by which the man was hanged, and which disappeared."

Suddenly seized with a fresh concern, he moved the red disk of the lantern over the walls. It revealed a tree trunk, which seemed quite alive. Then leaves . . . and branches that ran up the walls and disappeared into the ceiling. . . . There was a corner of a branch, and a leaf . . . then another leaf . . . then nothing but a ray of light that seemed to reflect itself. . . . Raoul passed his hand over the reflected light.

---

1. **Author's note:** These two pairs of shoes were never discovered. They must have been taken by a stage carpenter or door shutter.

He said, "The wall is a mirror."

"Yes," said the Persian and, passing his hand over his moist forehead, he added, "we have dropped into the torture chamber."

What the Persian knew of the torture chamber, and what became of the two companions there, shall be told in his own words.

21   Erik and the Persian

The Persian's Story: Part 1

It was the first time I entered the house on the lake. I had often begged the "trapdoor lover," as we used to call Erik in my country, to let me go in. He always refused.

One day, when I thought myself alone, I got into the boat and rowed toward the part of the wall through which I often saw Erik disappear. That is when I met the siren[1] who guarded the approach. Her charm was nearly fatal to me.

I was alone in the boat in the middle of the lake. Suddenly I was surrounded by a whispered singing that rose softly from the water. I leaned out of the little boat. The lake was perfectly calm and black as ink. I leaned out even further to enjoy the charm of the music. I leaned out until I almost overturned the boat.

Suddenly two monstrous arms rose up out of the water and seized me by the neck. They dragged me down to the depths with irresistible force. I would certainly have been lost if I had not had time to give a cry by which Erik knew me. It *was* Erik, and instead of drowning me, he pulled me to the bank.

"How foolish!" he said, standing over me dripping with water. "Why try to enter my house? I never

---

1. **siren** character in Greek mythology whose irresistible singing drew sailors to wreck their ships and perish on the rocks

invited you! I don't want you there, not anybody. Did you save my life just to make it unbearable?"

He spoke, but I only wanted to know how Eric had managed the trick.

He laughed and showed me a long reed. "It's a silly trick, but it's very useful for breathing and singing in the water."

I spoke to him severely:

"It is a trick that nearly killed me! And it may have killed others! You remember your promise to me, Erik? No more murders!"

"Have I really committed murders?" he asked, putting on his friendliest look.

"Remember you are responsible to me. If I had wished, there would be nothing more of you. Remember I saved your life! Tell me one thing, Erik . . . The chandelier . . . the chandelier, Erik?"

"What about the chandelier?"

"You know what I mean!"

"Oh!" he laughed, "that wasn't I! . . . The chandelier was very old and worn."

When Erik laughed, he was more terrible than ever. He jumped into the boat, chuckling so horribly that I shivered.

"Very old and worn, my dear daroga![2] It fell of itself! . . . It came down with a smash! . . . And now, daroga, take my advice and dry yourself. And never get into my boat again. And whatever you do, don't try to enter my house. I should be sorry to dedicate my Requiem Mass[3] to you!"

From that day, I gave up all thought of entering the

---

2. **daroga** Persian for "chief of police"
3. **Requiem Mass** Roman Catholic funeral service, often set to music

house through the lake. That entrance was too well guarded, especially now. But I thought there must be another entrance. I had often seen Erik disappear in the third cellar, but I didn't know how.

I soon discovered the curious relationship between the monster and Christine Daaé. Hiding in the lumber room[4] next to the young woman's dressing room, I listened. I heard the wonderful music that made Christine so ecstatic. Still I would never have thought that Erik's voice could make her forget his ugliness. I understood it all when I learned that Christine had not seen him!

I went to her dressing room and—remembering the lessons he taught me—I discovered the trick that made the mirror swing around. And I found the means, hollow bricks and so on, by which he made his voice carry to Christine as if it were beside her. In this way I also discovered the road that led to to the well and the dungeon—the Communists' dungeon[5]—and also the trapdoor that allowed Erik to go straight to the cellars below the stage.

A few days later I found the monster leaning over the well and sprinkling water on the forehead of Christine Daaé, who had obviously fainted. A white horse, the horse from *Prophète* was standing quietly beside them. I showed myself. It was terrible. Sparks flew from his yellow eyes. Before I had a chance to say a word, I received a blow to the head that stunned me.

When I came to, Erik, Christine, and the white

---

4. **lumber room** place where unused objects, such as furniture, are stored

5. **Communists' dungeon** place in the Opera House where members of the Commune imprisoned and killed many who opposed them

horse were gone. I was sure that the poor girl was a prisoner in the house on the lake. Without any hesitation, I went to the bank of the lake. I watched and waited, growing tired of the long waiting. I was beginning to think that he had gone through the other door on cellar three. But then I heard a light splashing in the dark, saw two yellow eyes shining like candles, and soon the boat touched shore. Erik jumped out and approached me:

"You've been out here for twenty-four hours," he said, "and you're annoying me. I tell you, this will all end badly. And it will be your fault. I have been very patient with you. You think you are following me, but it is I who am following you. I know all you know about me. I spared you yesterday *on the Communists' road*. But I warn you, don't let me catch you there again. You don't seem able to take a hint!

"Yes, you must learn—once and for all—to take a hint! You have already been arrested twice by the shade in the felt hat, who took you to the managers. They thought you were some eccentric Persian interested in stage mechanisms and life behind the scenes. I know all about that. I was there in the office. You know I am everywhere. They will wonder what you seek, and they will end up knowing you are after Erik . . . and then they will be after Erik themselves . . . and they'll discover the house on the lake. . . . If they do, it will be bad for you!. . . Anything could happen!

"It will be bad for a good number of the human race! That's all I have to tell you! Unless you are a great fool, it ought to be enough. . . . Except that you don't know how to take a hint!"

He had sat down on the stern of his boat. He was kicking his heels against its side, waiting for my response. I simply said:

"It's not Erik that I'm after!"

"Who then?"

"You know as well as I do: Christine Daaé," I answered.

"I have every right to see her in my own house. I am loved for my own sake," he retorted.

"That's not true," I said. "You have carried her off and are keeping her locked up."

"Listen," he said. "Will you promise never to meddle in my affairs again if I prove I am loved for my own sake?"

"Yes, I promise you," I replied with no hesitation. "I will believe you if Christine Daaé comes out of the house on the lake and returns to it of her own will."

To my astonishment, that is what happened. The young woman left the house on the lake and returned to it several times. She was not, apparently, forced to do so.

It was very hard for me to forget about Erik. The idea of a secret entrance in the third cellar haunted me. I went and waited for hours behind some scenery from *Roi de Lahore*. At last my patience was rewarded. One day I saw the monster approaching on his knees. I was sure he could not see me. He passed by and went to the wall. He pressed on a spring that moved a stone. He went through the hole and the stone closed behind him.

I was greatly interested in the relationship between Erik and Christine Daaé. I continued my wanderings around the Opera, and I soon learned the truth about the affair.

Erik filled Christine's mind through the terror with which he inspired her. But Christine's heart belonged wholly to the Vicomte Raoul de Chagny. They played like an innocent engaged couple, on the the upper floors of the Opera to avoid the monster. And they never suspected that someone was watching over them. I was prepared to do anything. I would kill the monster if necessary and explain to the police afterward. But Erik never showed himself. In spite of that I was never comfortable.

Several times, I went to the stone's hole and opened it. One day I heard astounding music. The monster was working on his *Don Juan Triumphant* with every door in the house open. He stopped playing, for a moment, and walked around like a madman.

"It must be finished *first*! All finished!"

The words concerned me. When the music started again, I closed the stone softly.

On the day Christine Daaé was kidnapped, I arrived at the theater rather late. I had worried all day, after reading the newspaper article suggesting an upcoming marriage between Christine and the Vicomte de Chagny. When I arrived at the Opera, I was almost astonished to see it still standing. I entered the theater, ready for any catastrophe.

Christine Daaé's abduction during the Prison Act astonished everyone else. But I was prepared for it. I was sure she had been whisked away by Erik, that prince of conjurers.[6] I thought this was the end of Christine—perhaps of everybody. I thought of advising everyone in the theater to escape at once, but I felt they would only think I was mad.

On the other hand, I resolved to act on my own. The chances were in my favor that Erik, at the moment, was only thinking about his captive. This would be the time to get into the house through the third cellar. I

6. conjurer someone who does magic, or sleight of hand tricks

decided to take with me that poor young fellow, the viscount. When I made the suggestion of that to him, he accepted with such confidence I was touched. I had sent my servant for my pistols. I gave one to the viscount and showed him how to hold himself ready to fire. After all, Erik could be waiting for us behind the wall. We set off to go down the Communists' road and through the trapdoor.

I did not have time to explain everything to the viscount. He is a brave fellow, but he knew nothing about this adversary. That was a good thing. My great fear was that he was already somewhere near us, preparing the Punjab lasso. No one knows better than he does how to throw the Punjab lasso. He is the king of the stranglers as well as the king of conjurers.

Erik had once lived in India, where he acquired incredible skill in the art of strangulation. He would have himself locked in a courtyard with a warrior, usually a man condemned to death. The man would be armed with a long pike and broadsword. Erik would have only his lasso. Just when the warrior thought he was going to take Erik with a tremendous blow, we would hear the lasso whistle through the air. With a little turn of the wrist, Erik would tighten the the wire around the warrior's neck and drag his victim to the audience.

This explains why I always made the viscount keep his hand at the level of his eyes. The pistols would actually serve no purpose, for Erik would never show himself. But I told M. de Chagny to keep his hand at the level of his eyes, with arm bent as though awaiting the command to fire. With his victim in this position, it would be impossible for even the most expert strangler to throw the lasso with advantage. It would catch you not only around the neck, but also around the arm or hand. This would allow you to easily unloose the lasso.

I knew Erik all too well to feel comfortable about jumping into his house. I knew what he had built in a certain palace at Mazenderan.[7] He was capable of astonishing inventions. Of these, the most horrible and dangerous was the torture chamber.

My alarm, therefore, was great when I saw that the room into which I and the viscount had dropped was an exact copy of the room at Mazenderan. At our feet I found the Punjab lasso which I had been dreading all evening. I was sure this rope had done duty for Joseph Buquet. The man probably caught Erik working the stone in the third cellar. He must have tried it, only to leave the room hanged. I can imagine Erik dragging the body to the scene from *Roi de Lahore* and hanging it there either as an example or to increase the superstitions that helped his interests. Then, on thinking more carefully, Eric probably went back to get the Punjab lasso. That lasso is made a special way and of catgut, and some policeman might have become too curious about it. This explains why the rope disappeared.

And now I had found the lasso, at our feet, in the torture chamber. I am no coward, but a cold sweat broke out on my forehead. I moved the red disc of my lantern across the walls.

M. de Chagny noticed my condition and asked:

"What is the matter, sir?"

I made a violent sign for him to be silent.

---

7. **Mazenderan** location in Persia where Erik designed the palace for the sultan who later ordered his death

22 *In the Torture Chamber*

The Persian's Story: Part 2

We were in a six-cornered room, the sides of which were covered with mirrors. I recognized the tree in the corner . . . the iron tree, with its iron branch, from which one could hang oneself.

I grabbed my companion's arm. He was very nervous, wanting only to call out to Christine. I was afraid he would not be able to control himself.

Suddenly there was a noise at our left. It sounded like a door opening and shutting. Then there was a moan.

"You must make your choice! The wedding mass or the requiem mass!"

I recognized the voice of the monster. There was another moan, followed by a long silence.

It was obvious that Erik did not know we were in the house. If he did, he would not have allowed us to hear him.

"The requiem mass is not at all happy," Erik's voice continued. "On the other hand, the wedding mass—take my word for it—is magnificent! You must make up your mind. I can't go on living like this, like a mole in a burrow. *Don Juan Triumphant* is finished. Now I want to live like everybody else. I want a wife, to take her out on Sundays. I've invented a mask that makes me look like everybody else. You'll be so happy! We'll sing, by ourselves, until we are exhausted. You are crying! You are afraid of me! And yet I am not bad.

Love me and you'll see! All I want is to be loved for myself. If you love me I'll be gentle as a lamb. You can do anything you want with me."

The moans increased, despairing. We recognized the moans as coming from Erik himself. Christine seemed to be struck dumb with horror. She seemed to have no strength to cry out, while the monster was on his knees before her.

"You don't love me! You don't love me! You don't love me!" Three times Erik wailed his fate. And then more gently:

"Why do you cry? You know it gives me pain to see you cry!"

Then silence.

Suddenly the silence was broken by an electric bell ringing.

A movement next door, then a sinister chuckle:

"Who has come calling now? Wait for me here. . . . I am going to tell the siren to answer the bell."

Footsteps moved away. A door closed. Christine was alone!

The Vicomte de Chagny was already calling:

"Christine! Christine!"

"I am dreaming," a soft voice said.

"Christine! Christine, it is I, Raoul!"

Then the soft voice whispered Raoul's name.

"Christine! It is not a dream, Christine! Trust me! . . . We are here to save you."

Christine told us in hurried words that Erik had gone mad. He had decided to kill everybody and himself if she did not consent to marry him. He had given her until eleven o'clock the next night to think about it. She must choose, as he said, between the wedding mass and the requiem. And then Erik said something Christine did not understand:

"Yes or no! If your answer is no, everybody will be dead *and buried.*"

I understood the sentence perfectly. It confirmed my worst fears.

Christine told us that Erik had left the house, but she could not check because she was tied. Both M. de Chagny and I gave a yell of anger. Our safety, the safety of Christine, all depended on her freedom of movement.

Christine described her room. She explained that there were only two doors. There was the door though which Erik came and went, as well as another locked door which he forbade her to enter—to the torture chamber.

"That is where we are, Christine!"

"You are in the torture chamber?"

"Mademoiselle, it is absolutely necessary for you to open that door for us!"

We heard her struggling, trying to free herself.

"I know where the key is," she said in a voice breathy from the effort she was making. "But I am tied so tightly. . . . It is in the next room, near the organ. It is with another little bronze key, which I am also forbidden to touch. They are in a small leather bag which he calls the bag of life or death. . . . Raoul! Leave here! Everything is so mysterious and terrible. Erik will soon have gone completely mad and you are in the torture chamber! . . . Go back the way you came."

I signed to Raoul to let me talk:

"Why did he tie you, mademoiselle? You cannot escape the house."

"I tried to commit suicide last night. He went out after bringing me here. He was going to *his banker,* he said. When he returned he found me. I had tried to kill myself by striking my forehead against the walls.

So he bound me. I am not allowed to die until tomorrow night at eleven o'clock."

"Mademoiselle, the monster tied you and he can untie you," I reminded her. "You only have to act the part. Remember that he loves you. Tell him the bonds hurt."

"Hush! I hear something in the wall by the lake. It is he! . . . Go away! Go away! Go away!"

"We cannot go away, even if we wanted to. We cannot leave here! And we are in the torture chamber!"

The sound of heavy steps finished conversation. They sounded behind the wall and then stopped, and made the floor creak once more. Next came a tremendous sigh, followed by a cry of horror from Christine."

"Why did you cry out, Christine?"

"Because I am in pain, Erik. Unloose my bonds. I am your prisoner; where will I go?"

"You will try to kill yourself again."

"No, Eric, you have given me until tomorrow night."

"I will release you, my dear. After all, as we are to die together. . . . I am as eager as you! . . . You have only to say one word, and *it will be all over for everybody!* You are right. You are right. Wait till eleven o'clock tomorrow night. We should think of ourselves in this life, and in death. The rest don't matter. *You are staring at me because I'm wet?* Oh, my dear, it's raining cats and dogs outside. . . . Apart from that, I think I'm subject to hallucinations. I beg your pardon for letting you see me in such a state. It's the other one's fault, however. Why did he ring? Do I ask people who pass to tell me the time? He'll never ask anyone again. It's the siren's fault, too. You know the man who rang the bell just now. . . . Go see if he's ringing at the bottom of the lake. . . . He was rather like. . . . There, turn around. . . . You're free now. . . . Your poor wrists! Have I hurt them? That alone deserves death! Speaking of death, *I must sing his requiem!*"

Who was the poor devil who had rung the bell and whose requiem would now be sung?

Erik sang like the god of thunder, enveloping us like a storm. Then the organ and the voice ceased so suddenly that M. de Chagny leaped back from the wall. And the voice, now changed and metallic, grated out:

"*What have you done with my bag?*"

23 *The Tortures Begin*

The Persian's Story: Part 3

The voice repeated angrily: "What have you done with my bag? So this is why you wanted to be untied? Don't you remember that it is the bag of life and death?"

We heard hurried steps, his chuckle, and Christine's cry of pain. Erik had apparently recovered his bag. At that moment the viscount could not hold back an exclamation.

"What's that sound?" said the monster. "Did you hear a cry?"

"I heard nothing. A cry? Are you going mad, Erik? Whom do you expect to cry, in this house? I cried out because you hurt me. I heard no other sound!"

"I don't like the way you said that. You're excited. . . . Why, you're trembling! . . . You're lying! There is someone here . . . someone in the torture chamber! . . . Ah! I understand now."

"There is no one, Erik!"

"I understand."

"No one!"

Another nasty chuckle. "Well, it won't take long to find out. Christine, we don't need to open the door to see. Would you like to see? Go up the folding steps. That's what they are there for. . . . They are to give a little peep into the torture chamber."

"What tortures? Who? . . . Erik, say you are only trying to frighten me! . . . Say it, if you love me! . . . There are no tortures, are there?"

"Go and look at the little window, dear. Go and peep through. Tell me what he looks like! . . . Up you go! How good of you to save me the exertion at my age! . . . Tell me! What does he look like?"

And that which I feared most began—we were suddenly flooded with light!

We heard the scraping of the steps being dragged against the wall, and then: "There is no one there, dear." We heard these words distinctly over our heads.

"Well, that's all right! What's the matter? You're not going to faint, are you? . . . as there's no one there. . . . Come down. . . . Pull yourself together. . . as there's no one there! *But how did you like the landscape?*"

"Very much!"

"What did you see?"

"I saw a forest."

"And what is in the forest?"

"Trees."

"And what is in a tree?"

"Birds."

"Did you see any birds?"

"No, I didn't see any birds."

"Well, what did you see? Think! Branches! And what are branches? Places from which to hang! That is why I call my wood the torture chamber! You see, it's all a joke. But I am tired of it! . . . I'm sick and tired of having a forest and a torture chamber in my house. And I'm tired of living in a house with a false bottom! I'm tired of it! I want a nice quiet apartment with ordinary doors and windows . . . with a wife in it, like anybody else. A wife I can keep amused. . . . Here, shall I show you some card tricks? That will help us pass some time while waiting for tomorrow night. . . . My dear little Christine, are you listening?. . . Tell me you love me! . . . No, you don't love me, but you will! . . .

One can get used to anything . . . if one wants to. And I will entertain you. What, you don't believe me? . . . I am the greatest ventriloquist in the world! . . . I am the first ventriloquist! . . . Listen!"

The monster was trying to divert her attention from us, but in vain. Gently she asked him over and over:

"Put out the light in the little window. . . . Erik, do put it out!"

She saw that the light meant something terrible.

But he began to play the ventriloquist:

"Here I raise my mask a little. See my lips, such as they are?. . . They're not moving! . . . My mouth is locked. Where would you like the voice? In your left ear? Right? In the table? In those boxes on the fireplace? There it is in the little box on the left. *Shall I turn the grasshopper?* Now it's in the little leather bag. *I am the bag of life and death!* Now it is in Carlotta's throat. What does it say? 'It's I, Mr. Toad. I'm singing! *I feel without alarm—co-ack—with its melody enwind me— co-ack!'* And now it's in the ghost's chair, and it says, *'Madame Carlotta is singing tonight to bring down the chandelier!'* Where is Erik's voice now? Listen, Christine, darling! Listen! It's in the torture chamber! And what do I say? *'Woe to them that have a nose, a real nose, and come to look around!* Aha, aha, aha!' "

The voice was everywhere. It came through the little window and through the walls. It ran around us, between us. And then it stopped, for this is what happened:

"Erik, Erik! You tire me with the voice! Isn't it very hot here?"

"Oh, yes," replied Erik's voice. "It is unbearably hot in here!"

"What does that mean? . . . The wall is getting very

hot! . . . The wall is burning! . . ."

"I'll tell you, Christine: it's coming from the forest next door."

"*What does that have to do with it? The forest?*"

"Didn't you see that it was an African forest?"

And the monster laughed so loudly we could not distinguish Christine's cries from the laughter. The Vicomte de Chagny shouted and beat on the walls like a madman. I could not restrain him. But we heard only the monster's laughter, and he could not have heard anything else. And then there was the sound of a body falling onto the floor and being dragged along. A door slammed and then nothing. Nothing more except the scorching silence of the tropics, in the heart of a tropical forest.

24

"Barrels! Barrels!
Any Barrels to Sell?"

The Persian's Story: Part 4

I have said that the torture room was a regular
hexagon, and the walls were lined entirely with mirrors. There was, therefore, nothing to take hold of.
There was no furniture. The ceiling could be lit up.
And a system of electric heating allowed the tempera-
ture of the walls and room to be controlled at will. In
one corner there was an iron tree on a rotating stage.
The tree, with its painted leaves, was absolutely true
to life. Made of iron, it was indestructible. The mirrors multiplied it a thousand times. These details all
together produced the illusion of an equatorial forest
blazing under the tropical sun.

In addition, the tree could be rotated to change the
scene to that of a desert, or worse still, the mirage of
an oasis.

When the ceiling lit up and the forest became visible, the viscount was stunned. He rubbed his eyes and
blinked, and for a moment he forgot to listen. I, having
seen this invention of Erik's before, was not at all surprised at the sight of the forest. Therefore, I was able
to listen for both of us. Also, my attention was attracted
to the mirrors. They were broken here and there and
in the corners. This proved to me that the torture
chamber had *already served a purpose.*

Yes, someone, mad with rage, had kicked at the
mirrors to escape his agony. The branch of the tree

where he put an end to his suffering was positioned in such a way that he would have seen a thousand men hanging with him.

Yes, I was sure Joseph Buquet had been through all this. Were we to die as he had done? I did not think so, because we had some hours of time and I knew how to use them. After all, I was familiar with most of Erik's "tricks," and now was the time to use my knowledge.

There was only one possible way out. The passage through which we had jumped was inaccessible. It was much too high, completely out of reach. There was only the door into the room where Erik and Christine Daaé were. It was invisible to us, so we had to try to open it without knowing where it was. And now that it was clear Christine would be unable to help us, I resolved we should set to work right away.

First I had to calm M. de Chagny, who was pacing like a madman, muttering. The conversation he had overheard between Christine and the monster had, understandably, upset him terribly. Added to that were the magic forest and the scorching heat. He shouted Christine's name, banged his head against the glass, and waved the pistol about. In other, words, the torture was beginning to work on him.

I tried reason. I made him touch the mirrors and the tree:

"Look, we are in a little room. Keep saying that to yourself. And we shall leave the room as soon as we find the door."

And I promised him that if he could be still, I would discover the trick of the door in less than one hour.

He lay on the floor, said the view was splendid from there, and said he would wait for me. The torture was working on him in spite of my efforts.

Myself, I set to work. I took one glass panel and touched every inch of it in all directions. I was searching for a weak point where I would find the spring to pivot the door. I knew it would be no higher than my hands could reach. Erik was about my height, and he would not place the spring out of his own reach. I worked as fast as I could, for the heat was becoming unbearable. In a half hour, I had examined three panels. Then, the viscount began to talk. I looked at him to see his condition. In doing so, I lost my place on the panels and had to begin again at random, feeling and groping.

Now the fever took hold of me. I could find nothing. The room was silent. We were lost in a forest, without a compass, guide, or anything helpful. I knew what would happen to us if I could not find the spring. But I found only branches, beautiful branches from which there was no shade.

M. de Chagny seemed quite "gone." He thought he had been walking in the forest for three days and nights. He called to Christine in such a sorrowful voice that it brought tears to my eyes.

I went on hunting, hunting for the spring. Evening was coming, and darkness falls quickly in the tropics—quickly, with no twilight. The heat did not go when the daylight went. If anything, it seemed hotter. I urged the viscount to hold his pistol ready and not to stray from camp, while I continued the search.

Suddenly there was the roar of a lion only a few yards away.

"Oh!" whispered the viscount. "It is very close. . . . Do you see him?. . . There . . . through the trees! . . . If he roars again, I'll fire at him!"

The roaring did come again, louder. And the viscount fired. Only he smashed a mirror, as I discovered at daybreak.

I was surprised no other dangerous animals came. Usually after the lion comes the leopard and the buzzing tsetse fly. I explained to my young companion how Erik made the noises. Talking about Erik made me decide to talk with him. We had to give up any idea of surprising him, and he must know who was in the torture chamber. I called to him.

I shouted as loudly as I could, across the desert, but there was no answer. All around us lay silence and the vastness of the stony desert. We were so thirsty! I saw M. de Chagny raise up on one elbow and point to a spot on the horizon. He had discovered an oasis!

It was a mirage. I recognized it at once. No one would have been able to resist it. I tried not to hope for water. I knew if I did, there would be only one choice after striking only mirrors: to hang myself on the iron tree. So I cried to the viscount:

"It is the mirage! The mirage! Do not believe in the water! It is another trick of the mirrors!"

He flatly told me to shut up, with my explanations and my revolving doors and my illusions. He dragged himself toward it, saying:

"Water! Water!"

His mouth was open, as though he were drinking. And my mouth was open, too, as though I were drinking. We not only saw the water; we heard it ripple. A sound you hear with your tongue!

Lastly, we heard the rain. It was not raining. I knew how Erik could be making the sound. We put out our tongues and dragged ourselves toward the river bank. When we reached the mirror, M. de Chagny licked it. . . . And so did I.

It was burning hot! As we writhed in pain, the viscount put the pistol to his brain. I noticed the tree had returned, and I knew for whom it waited. But as I stared at the Punjab lasso, I saw something that made me jump. M. de Chagny stopped in the midst of his suicide attempt. I caught his arm, took the pistol from him . . . and dragged myself toward the lasso.

Near it, I saw a groove in the floor and, in it, a black-headed nail. I had found the spring! I felt the nail. It yielded to my pressure. A cellar flap released in the floor. Cool air came up from the black hole below. I thrust my arm into the darkness. There was a stone and another . . . a staircase . . . a dark staircase leading into the cellar. Fearing a new trick of the monster, I took the dark lantern and went down first.

At the bottom, there were shapes, circular shapes . . . on which I turned the light of my lantern.

Barrels!

We were in Erik's cellar. It was here he kept his wine and perhaps his drinking water. Erik was a lover of good wine. And there was plenty here!

There were quite a number of barrels, stacked neatly in two rows. They were small barrels, and I thought that Erik must have chosen them for ease in carrying them to the house on the lake.

We examined them. All were sealed. Then after lifting one to be sure it was full, I prepared to break one open.

At that moment we heard singing:

"Barrels! Barrels! Any barrels to sell?"

The song seemed to come from inside the barrels.

But then we heard nothing more, so we returned to the work of opening the barrel. M. de Chagny put his two hands underneath it and, with an effort, I broke it open.

"What's this? This isn't water!"

I stooped to look and at once threw the lantern
away with such force that it broke and went out, leaving us in total darkness.

What I had seen in M. de Chagny's hands was
gunpowder!

25 *The Scorpion or the Grasshopper?*

The Persian's Story: Part 5

The discovery of the gunpowder threw us into such a state of alarm that we forgot our recent suffering. Now we knew what the monster meant when he said to Christine Daaé:

"Yes or no! If your answer is no, everybody will be dead *and buried!*"

Buried under the Grand Opera of Paris.

The monster had chosen eleven o'clock because there would be many people, many "members of the human race," up there in the theater. What finer attendance for his funeral? He would go to his death escorted by Paris's best-dressed theatergoers!

We were to be blown up in the middle of the performance . . . if Christine Daaé said no!

We dragged ourselves through the dark, feeling for the stone steps. I stopped, a terrible thought in mind: what time was it? . . . Who could tell? We could have been in the tropical forest for days! And then, a sound. A crack!

M. de Chagny and I began to yell like crazy people. And we rushed up the staircase, stumbling, running to escape the dark. We returned to the torture room, which was as dark as the cellar that we had just left. We shouted: M. de Chagny to Christine, and I to Erik. I reminded him that I had saved his life. No answer. My watch had stopped, but de Chagny's was still running. He broke the glass of his watch to feel the hands.

He thought it was just eleven o'clock. Perhaps it was not the final eleven o'clock. Perhaps we still had twelve hours.

I heard footsteps next door. Someone tapped on the wall. Christine Daaé's voice said:

"Raoul! Raoul!"

We all talked at once on both sides of the wall. The monster had been terrible! He had done nothing but rave, waiting for the "yes" that she had refused to give. She promised to give her "yes" if Erik would take her to the torture chamber. He had refused and had uttered hideous threats against the whole human race. At last, he had gone out to let her reflect for the last time.

"What time is it, Christine?"

"It is eleven o'clock, all but five minutes! The eleven o'clock which is to decide life or death. He told me so just before he left. He is quite mad! He tore off his mask, and his eyes shot flames! He did nothing but laugh. He said, 'I give you five minutes to spare your blushes! Here is the little bronze key that opens the two ebony caskets on the mantel. In one casket is a scorpion; in the other a grasshopper. Make your choice before I return. If you turn the scorpion around, that will mean yes to me. The grasshopper will mean no.' He laughed like a drunken devil. I begged him for the key to the torture chamber, but he said it was not necessary. He was going to throw it in the lake. He laughed again. His last words were, 'The grasshopper! Be careful of the grasshopper! It not only can turn; it hops! It hops very high!' "

The five minutes were almost past. I thought about what Erik had said. The grasshopper . . . turns . . . hops . . . and with it, many people. No doubt the grasshopper was connected to an electric current intended to blow up the gunpowder.

M. de Chagny seemed to have recovered his moral energy from hearing Christine's voice. He told her to turn the scorpion at once. I cried:

"Christine, where are you?"

"By the scorpion."

"Do not touch it!"

The idea had come to me that Erik would try to deceive the young woman. Perhaps the scorpion would blow everything up. After all, where was he? Perhaps he had taken shelter and was waiting for the explosion! He could not really expect Christine to ever consent to become his prey!

We heard steps approaching. He came up to Christine but did not speak. I shouted:

"Erik! It is I! Do you know me?"

With great calm, he replied at once:

"So you're not dead in there? Well, then see that you keep quiet! The honor rests with mademoiselle. . . . Mademoiselle has not touched the scorpion, and mademoiselle has not touched the grasshopper. There, I open the caskets without a key, since I am the trap-door lover. I can open and shut what I please. Look at these dears inside. Aren't they pretty? There is enough gunpowder under our feet to blow up a whole quarter of Paris. If you turn the scorpion, all that powder will be soaked and drowned. You shall make a handsome present to a few hundred Parisians upstairs . . . their lives. Turn the scorpion and merrily, merrily, we will be married."

"Erik, do you swear that the scorpion is the one to turn?"

"Yes, to hop at our wedding."

"You said 'hop'!"

"At our wedding! That is enough! You won't turn the scorpion? Then I turn the grasshopper!"

"Erik, I have turned the scorpion!"

Something cracked, then there was a terrible hiss through the trapdoor. It sounded like the hiss of a rocket.

It came softly at first, then louder. It was not the hiss of fire. It was more a gurgle now. A gurgle!

We rushed to the trapdoor. The water rose in the cellar, above the barrels. "Barrels! Barrels! Any barrels to sell?" We bent down to it and drank. We stood on the floor of the cellar and drank. We went up the stairs, one by one, and drank. Up came the water. There was surely enough now. There would be enough soon to flood the whole house on the lake. Erik must turn off the tap!

"Erik! Erik! Turn off the tap! Turn off the scorpion!"

But there was no answer. We heard nothing but the rising water. It was halfway to our waists!

"Christine!" cried the viscount.

But Christine did not reply. We heard nothing. No one in the next room. No one to turn the scorpion! We were all alone, in the dark, with the freezing dark water rising around us.

"Erik! Erik!"

"Christine! Christine!"

By now we had lost our footing and were spinning around in the water. It turned us and threw us against the mirrors, which threw us back again. Were we to die here, drowned in the torture chamber? I had not foreseen that. Erik had never shown me that.

My hands felt the trunk of the iron tree. I called the viscount, and we both clung to the branch of the tree. The water rose higher and higher. We had to release the tree. Our arms got entangled in the effort of swimming. We choked, we fought the dark water, we could hardly breathe the dark air above it. We could hear the air escaping through some vent hole, somewhere.

"Turn until you find the air hole, then glue your mouth to it!"

But I lost my strength. The walls were too slippery. We whirled around again and again! We began to sink! One last effort! A last cry:

"Erik! Christine!"

The gurgling in our ears . . . then, before losing consciousness, I seemed to hear:

"Barrels! Barrels! Any barrels to sell?"

26 *The End of the Ghost's Love Story*

The last chapter ended the written narrative the Persian left behind him. Although they seemed doomed, M. de Chagny and his companion were saved by the devotion of Christine Daaé. I heard the rest of the story from the lips of the daroga himself.

When I went to see him, he was still living in his old apartment, but he was very ill. I had to use all my powers of persuasion as an historian to get him to relive the incredible tragedy for me. Darius, his faithful servant, let me in. The daroga sat by a window looking over the Tuileries.[1] He told me his story.

When the Persian opened his eyes, he was lying on a bed and M. de Chagny was on a sofa nearby. An angel and a devil were watching over them.

Christine Daaé did not say a word. She moved about like a sister of charity who had taken a vow of silence. She brought a cup of tea. The man in the mask took it from her hands and brought it to the Persian himself. M. de Chagny was still sleeping.

"He awakened a long time before we knew if you were alive, daroga. He is quite well and sleeping. We won't disturb him."

Erik left the room and the Persian raised himself on his elbow. He called to Christine who was sitting by the window. She came and laid her hand on his forehead then went away again. He noticed that she did

---

1. **the Tuileries** a beautiful, large garden in Paris

not look at M. de Chagny, but sat down again in her chair by the window.

Erik came back with some little bottles, which he placed on the mantel. In a whisper, so as not to wake M. de Chagny, he said:

"You are both saved now. And soon, I shall take you up to the surface, *to please my wife.*"

Saying this, he rose and left the room again.

The Persian looked at Christine again. She was reading a tiny book, with gilt edges, perhaps a religious book. He called to her again, but Christine was wrapped up in her book and did not hear him.

Soon the Persian fell asleep again, and did not awaken until he was in his own room. He learned from his servant Darius that he had been found propped against the door to the apartment. Someone had put him there, rung the bell, then gone away.

When he had regained his strength, he sent a message to the de Chagnys' house to inquire about the brothers. He was told the younger brother had not been seen and that Count Philippe was dead. His body had been found on the bank of the Opera lake. The Persian remembered the requiem mass he had heard played. There was no doubt concerning the crime and the criminal. Obviously the Count had dashed off thinking he was in pursuit of Raoul and Christine. When he discovered his error, he must have remembered Raoul's belief about his strange rival. He went in search of him in the cellars. That was enough to explain the body at the shore where the siren kept watch.

Determined to inform the police, the Persian went to Faure, the examining magistrate. Faure took down his statement and treated him like a madman. Thus frustrated, he began to write his story. Perhaps the press would be glad of it. Just as he had finished the lines just quoted in the previous chapters, Darius announced a visitor. The visitor had refused to give his name, but would not leave without seeing the daroga. The Persian at once ordered the visitor sent in. As he thought, it was Erik!

Erik was extremely weak and leaned against the wall to keep from falling. Taking off his hat, he revealed a forehead white as wax. The rest of his face was hidden by a mask.

The Persian rose and greeted Erik:

"Murderer of Count Philippe, what have you done with his brother and with Christine Daaé?"

Erik, stunned by this direct attack, dragged himself into a chair and heaved a great sigh. Then speaking in short phrases and gasping for breath between the words:

"Daroga, don't talk to me . . . about Count Philippe. . . . He was dead . . . when . . . the siren sang. . . . It was an . . . accident . . . a sad . . . a very sad . . . accident. . . . He fell . . . into the lake!"

"You lie!" shouted the Persian.

Erik bowed his head and said:

"I have not come here . . . to talk about anyone . . . but to tell you that . . . I am going . . . to die."

"Where are Raoul de Chagny and Christine Daaé?"

"I am going . . . to die. . . ."

"Raoul de Chagny and Christine Daaé?"

"Of love, daroga . . . I am dying . . . of love. . . . That is how it is. . . . I loved her so! . . . I love her still . . . daroga . . . and I am dying of love for her. . . . I tell you! . . . If you knew how beautiful she was . . . when she let me kiss her . . . alive. . . . It was the first time . . . the first time . . . I ever kissed a woman. . . . Yes, alive. . . I kissed her alive . . . and she looked as beautiful as if she . . . had been dead. . . ."

The Persian shook Erik by the arm. "Will you tell me if she is dead or alive! Is she dead now?"

"I tell you I kissed her on her forehead . . . and she did not draw back from my lips ! . . . Oh, she is a good girl! . . . As to her being dead, I don't think so. . . . But it has nothing to do with me! . . . No! No! She is not dead! . . . And no one shall touch a hair on her head! . . . She is a good, honest girl . . . and she saved your life, daroga . . . at a moment when I would have let you die! . . . Why were you there?. . . Why were you with that little fellow?. . . You could have died as well as he. . . . My word, she begged for his life! But I told her that since she had turned the scorpion, she was engaged to me . . . not to him!

"As for you, you have Christine to thank. You were yelling like the devil. The water was rising. She came to me with her beautiful eyes open. She swore she had consented to be my living wife. She wanted to live! Until then I had always seen her as my dead wife. She wanted to live! She would not commit suicide! It was a bargain. . . . It was understood that I was to take both of you up to the surface. I took you, and I came back alone. . . ."

"What have you done with the Vicomte de Chagny?" interrupted the Persian.

"I couldn't carry him up like you, at once. He was a hostage. . . . But I couldn't keep him at the house because of Christine. . . . So I locked him up comfortably in the Communists' dungeon. I chained him nicely. . . . A whiff of Mazenderan scent had left him limp as a rag.

"When I came back, Christine was waiting for me . . . a real, living bride. . . . And, when I . . . came forward like a timid child . . . she did not run away . . . no, no . . . she stayed . . . she waited for me . . . I even believe,

daroga. . . that she put out her forehead . . . a little . . .
oh, not much . . . just a little . . . like a living bride. . . .
And . . . and . . . I . . . kissed her! I! . . . I! . . . I! . . . And
she did not die! . . . How good it is, daroga . . . to kiss
someone on the forehead! . . . You don't know! . . . My
mother, daroga, my poor unhappy mother would never
. . . let me kiss her. . . . She would run away . . . and
throw me my mask! . . . Nor any other woman . . . ever,
ever! My happiness was so great, I cried. And I fell at
her feet, crying. . . I kissed her little feet . . . crying.
You're crying, too, daroga . . . and she cried also . . . the
angel cried."

Erik sobbed aloud and the Persian himself could
not hold back his tears in the presence of the masked
man who was moaning in pain and love, by turns.

"I felt her tears on my forehead . . . on mine, on
mine! . . . They were soft and sweet! . . . They trickled
under my mask . . . and they mingled with mine. . . .
Listen, daroga, to what I did. . . . I tore off my mask so
as not to lose one tear . . . and she did not run away! . . .
And she did not die! . . . She wept with me. We cried
together! . . . I have tasted all the happiness the world
can offer!

"I had in my hand a ring, a plain gold ring . . .
which I had given her . . . and which she had lost, and
which I found again. I gave it to her and said, 'There . . .
take it! . . . It will be my wedding present! . . . I know
you love the boy . . . don't cry anymore!' I told her I
knew I was only a poor dog to her, ready to die for her
. . . but she should marry the young man she loved . . .
when she pleased, because she had cried with me. . . .

"I released the young man," Erik continued, "and I
told him to come with me to Christine. . . . They kissed
in front of me. . . . Christine had my ring. I made
Christine promise to come back one night when I was

dead. She is to bury me in the greatest secrecy with the gold ring. I told her where to find my body and what to do with it. Then Christine kissed me, for the first time, herself. Here on the the forehead . . . on my forehead . . . mine! If Christine keeps her promise, daroga, she will be back soon!"

The Persian asked no questions. No one would have doubted Erik's word that night.

The monster collected his energy to leave. He told the Persian that he would send him something, in gratitude for the kindness which the Persian had once shown him. The something was what he held dearest in the world: all Christine's papers that she had written for Raoul and left with Erik.

In reply to the Persian's question, Erik told him that the two young people—as soon as they had found themselves free—had decided to go find a priest. They went to some lonely spot where they could hide their happiness from the public. Lastly, Erik relied on the Persian to inform the young couple of his death and to advertise it in the *Epoque*.

That was all. The Persian saw him to the door, and Darius put him in a cab. He said to the driver:

"Take me to the Opera."

The cab drove off into the night. The Persian had seen the monster for the last time. Three weeks later, the *Epoque* published this notice:

"Erik is dead."

Epilogue

You can see why it is impossible to deny that Erik actually lived. The proof is within the reach of everyone. The case was very exciting. Kidnapping, deaths, disappearances, druggings. . . . One of the most fascinating mysteries was what had become of the wonderful Christine Daaé. She was portrayed as the victim of a rivalry between two brothers. No one knows that Christine and Raoul withdrew to enjoy a happiness they did not want to make public after the strange death of Count Philippe. They took the train from "the northern railway station of the world." Possibly I will one day look around Scandinavia for some traces of them and also of Mme. Valérius, who disappeared at the same time!

The Persian alone knew the whole truth and possessed papers that proved it. He helped me finish the proof. I kept in contact with him daily. He directed my activities. He had amazing recollections of the Opera house and its secret recesses. He also directed me to people who had information.

He sent me to call on the retired manager, M. Poligny, to ask about the Opera ghost. Poligny acted as if I were the devil himself. When I related this to the Persian, he said that Poligny, being superstitious by nature, was first convinced he had heard a voice from Heaven. Then, when the voice asked for money, he saw that he was being victimized by a blackmailer. Both Debienne and Poligny had tired of managing the Opera. So they retired and left the whole mystery to the next directors.

Moncharmin was also puzzling. I was surprised that in his *Memoirs of a Manager* he mentions the ghost at length in the first part of the book and hardly at all in the rest of it. The Persian reminded me of the simple way the famous incident of the 20,000 francs was dismissed. The money had turned up on Richard's table with a note inscribed in red ink, "*With O. G.'s compliments.*" Moncharmin continued to believe Richard had played a joke on him. For his part, Richard continued to believe Moncharmin had invented the whole affair of the Opera ghost to get even for a few past jokes. The Persian suggested I could figure out the mystery if I would look in the managers' office and remember that Erik was nicknamed the *trapdoor lover.*

The important papers related to the mystery include the Persian's manuscript, as well as the statements made to me by people who used to work for MM. Richard and Moncharmin, by little Meg Giry (the worthy Madame Giry is no more), and by Sorelli—who is retired. All the documents about the existence of the ghost have been checked and confirmed by some discoveries of which I am very proud. I have not been able to find the house on the lake.[1] Erik blocked up all the secret entrances. On the other hand, I *have* found the secret passage of the Communists, and also the trapdoor through which Raoul and the Persian got down into the cellars. In the Communists' dungeon, I found initials carved on the walls. Among these were an "R" and an "C." R.C.: Raoul de Chagny. The letters are still there.

---

1. **Author's note:** Even so, I am convinced it could be found by draining the lake. Who knows? Perhaps the score of *Don Juan Triumphant* might be discovered in the house?

If you will visit the Opera one morning without a guide, go to Box 5 and knock with your fist or stick on the enormous column. There is space inside it to hold two men. And, if you think the column is on the wrong side, remember the ghost was an excellent ventriloquist.

The most important discovery was in the managers' office. I found it in the presence of the acting manager. It is just a couple of inches from the desk chair. There is a trapdoor the width of a floor board, and the length of a man's forearm. It is easy to imagine a hand coming out the lid of the trapdoor and fumbling easily at the pocket of a coat. It is through this trap door that the 40,000 francs went, and the way by which they were returned.

When I talked to the Persian about the lease, I suggested Erik might have been simply amusing himself.

"Don't you believe it!" the Persian replied. "Erik wanted money. And he thought he should be compensated for his ugliness. When he returned the money, it was because he no longer wanted it. He had given up his marriage to Christine Daaé, and so he gave up everything above the surface of the earth."

According to the Persian, Erik was born in a small town not far from Rouen.[2] His father was a master mason. He ran away at an early age, because his ugliness was a source of terror for his family. From time to time, he let himself be exhibited at fairs as "the living corpse." Living among the Gypsies, he became an artist and a magician. He sang like no one else, and he practiced ventriloquism. He gave

---

2. **Rouen** city and port in Northern France, on the Seine River

extraordinary displays of "sleight of hand." It was through this that he became known in the Persian palace of Mazenderan. A fur dealer told of the marvels he had seen performed in Erik's tent. The trader was summoned to the palace, and the daroga of Mazenderan questioned him. The daroga was then told to find Erik. He brought him to Persia, where Erik became very powerful. He was guilty of some horrors, for he didn't seem to know the difference between good and evil. He took part in some political assassinations and the Shah took a liking to him.

Erik had some original ideas about architecture. He thought about buildings the way a conjuror uses a trick casket. The Shah ordered him to build a palace of this kind. Erik did so, and the Shah was apparently able to go about unseen—disappearing at will. When the Shah saw his gem of a palace, he ordered Erik's eyes to be put out so he could never build another like it. However, he knew that, even blind, Erik would be able to design. So long as Erik lived, his secret was not safe. The daroga was ordered to kill Erik and all the laborers who had worked under his direction. In payment for some past favors, the daroga gave Erik a means of escape, for which he almost paid with his life.

A corpse, half eaten by birds of prey, was found on the shore of the Caspian Sea. The daroga's friends dressed the corpse in Erik's clothes and identified the body accordingly. The daroga was banished from the country, and he went to live in Paris.

Erik went first to Asia Minor and then to Constantinople, where he pleased the Sultan. He built trapdoors and secret chambers for the Sultan's palace. Of course, he soon had to leave the Sultan's services. It was for the same reason he had to leave Persia: he knew too much! Tired of his adventurous but monstrous life, Erik longed to be like everybody else. He became a contractor, building ordinary houses with ordinary bricks. He made a bid on part of the foundations of the Opera. His estimate was accepted. Soon he found himself in the cellars of an enormous playhouse. His magician's nature took over. He dreamed of creating, for himself, a dwelling unknown to the rest of the world, where he could hide from people's eyes.

You know the rest. Poor, unhappy Erik! Shall we pity him? Shall we curse him? He only wanted to be like everybody else. But he was too ugly! He either had to hide his genius or *use it play tricks with*, when with an ordinary face, he would have been a most distinguished person. He had to be content with a cellar—though no ordinary cellar!

I have prayed that God might show his mercy, his crimes notwithstanding. I am sure that I prayed over his body when they took it from the spot where they were burying the phonograph records. It was his skeleton. I did not recognize it from the ugliness of his head. Everyone is ugly when dead for so long. I recognized it from the plain gold ring he wore. Christine Daaé had certainly slipped it on his finger when she came to bury him as she had promised.

The skeleton was lying near the little well. It was the spot where the Angel of Music first held Christine in his arms. And now where will the skeleton go? To a common grave? It is no ordinary skeleton. The place for it is in the archives of the National Academy of Music.

REVIEWING
YOUR READING

Chapters 1-2

FINDING THE MAIN IDEA

1. Box 5 is not to be sold because
    (A) the managers use it (B) the ghost uses it (C) Count
    de Chagny uses it (D) the undersecretary uses it.
2. The descriptions of the ghost include
    (A) a death's head (B) evening clothes (C) a head of fire.
    (D) all of these

REMEMBERING DETAILS

3. The reason for the gala at the Opera is
    (A) a performance of *Faust* (B) Christine's debut
    (C) the managers' retirement (D) a celebration of notable
    musicians.
4. Meg Giry, Little Jammes, and the others in La Sorelli's
    dressing room are:
    (A) singers (B) understudies (C) stage managers and
    scene-changers (D) ballerinas.
5. Christine Daaé sang at the gala because
    (A) La Carlotta was sick (B) the managers liked her
    (C) she was a star (D) it pleased the influential de Chagny
    family.

DRAWING CONCLUSIONS

6. Meg Giry's mother knows a lot about the ghost because
    (A) she has seen him (B) Joseph Buquet told her
    (C) she gives him his program. (D) all of these

USING YOUR REASON

7. Philippe concludes that Raoul is interested in Christine
    because
    (A) he knows his way to her dressing room (B) Raoul tells
    him (C) Raoul talks of marrying soon (D) Raoul gives her
    flowers.

   8. Christine said, "I gave you my soul tonight." What opera
   did she sing music from? How does Christine's comment
   coincide with the music she sang? To whom do you think
   Christine was talking?

Chapters 3-4

FINDING THE MAIN IDEA
   1. MM. Moncharmin and Richard think that the ghost is a figment of the imaginations of
   (A) Debienne and Poligny (B) *le corps de ballet*
   (C) La Carlotta (D) a friend.

REMEMBERING DETAILS
   2. The ghost's wishes are written up in
   (A) a set of notes in Box 5 (B) a letter from the ghost
   (C) an addition to the Opera lease (D) the newspaper.
   3. The ghost writes in what color of ink?
   (A) red (B) blue (C) black (D) brown
   4. Mme. Giry works as a
   (A) wardrobe lady (B) dresser (C) shopkeeper
   (D) boxkeeper.
   5. Richard can best be described as
   (A) funny (B) short tempered (C) selfish (D) quiet.

DRAWING CONCLUSIONS
   6. When Richard and Moncharmin listen to the stories of the
   Inspector and Mme. Giry, their reaction can best be
   described as
   (A) amused (B) disbelieving (C) frightened (D) bored.

USING YOUR REASON
   7. Moncharmin and Richard think that the stories of the ghost are
   (A) an old story (B) a practical joke (C) too scary to talk
   about (D) too serious.

THINKING IT OVER
   8. The retiring managers, Debienne and Poligny, said that any
   time they ignored the wishes of the ghost something bad
   happened. The ghost did not want to be discussed. What
   might these facts have to do with Joseph Buquet's death?

Chapter 5

1. Raoul gets very impatient with Christine about the Angel of Music because
    (A) he is jealous (B) he is very young (C) she will not marry him (D) she sings poorly for everyone else.
2. Christine believed the Angel of Music was
    (A) her father (B) sent by the Opera ghost (C) sent by her father (D) a real person.

REMEMBERING DETAILS
3. Christine went to Perros because it was
    (A) where she met Raoul (B) the anniversary of her father's death (C) on the water (D) where the Angel lived.
4. At midnight in the graveyard, Christine and Raoul heard
    (A) violin music (B) beautiful singing (C) the korrigans dancing (D) the ghost of Christine's father.

DRAWING CONCLUSIONS
5. Christine was surprised that Raoul had heard the voice in her dressing room, probably because
    (A) she was joking (B) he was joking (C) she thought he had left (D) she thought nobody else could hear the voice.

USING YOUR REASON
6. Raoul knew that he could not marry Christine because
    (A) she loved her music too much (B) she was not of the same aristocratic class (C) she had vowed not to marry (D) her father would be left alone.

IDENTIFYING THE MOOD
7. The author probably included korrigans in his story to
    (A) complicate the story (B) heighten the supernatural atmosphere (C) prove that Christine will believe anything. (D) none of the above

Chapters 6-7

FINDING THE MAIN IDEA
1. The ghost warned that a catastrophe would occur. Which of the following things happened during the performance?

(A) The lake overflowed. (B) Joseph Buquet died.
(C) Carlotta's forgot her part. (D) The chandelier fell on
the audience.

REMEMBERING DETAILS

2. The Opera ghost does not want Carlotta to sing because
(A) he wants Christine to sing (B) Carlotta brings bad luck
(C) Carlotta is sick (D) he hates her.
3. Carolus Fonta is
(A) a stage manager (B) Richard's concierge (C) a tenor
singer (D) the missing scene-changer.
4. Carlotta's friends came to the Opera to cheer her because
(A) Carlotta was afraid her voice was bad (B) they thought
that Christine Daaé was going to do something bad to
Carlotta (C) the ghost had told them to come (D) they
wanted to hear *Faust.*

DRAWING CONCLUSIONS

5. The two managers check out Box 5 themselves because of
(A) stories told by the previous managers (B) Mme. Giry's
story (C) the Inspector's report about what happened in
the box the night before (D) the theft of the horse César.

USING YOUR REASON

6. Firmin Richard fired Mme. Giry because
(A) she was not a good worker (B) he thought she was
crazy (C) she boxed him on the ear (D) he thought her
dishonest.
7. Carlotta thought Christine had cooked up a plot against her
so that
(A) Christine could sing (B) Carlotta would be fired
(C) Count Philippe would notice Christine (D) Carolus
Fonta would sponsor Christine.

THINKING IT OVER

8. The Opera ghost needed to convince the new managers
that he was real. In this scene, he made his presence felt
by several actions. What did he do? Were the managers
convinced?

Chapters 8-10

FINDING THE MAIN IDEA

1. Christine met the Angel of Music at Perros because
   (A) she wanted him to see her father's grave (B) she wanted
   Raoul to meet the Angel (C) he promised to play music on
   her father's violin (D) she hoped he would appear to her.

REMEMBERING DETAILS

2. Madame Valérius said that the Angel of Music forbids
   Christine to marry by
   (A) telling her he loves her (B) telling her he will leave
   her if she marries (C) telling her a catastrophe will happen
   if she marries. (D) all of these

3. The Comte de Chagny had news of Christine after she disappeared. She was seen
   (A) driving a car (B) riding on the lake (C) riding in a
   carriage through the park (D) at the ballet.

4. Christine told Raoul that the gold ring she wore was a
   (A) present (B) a friendship ring (C) a wedding ring from
   the Angel (D) a gift from her father.

DRAWING CONCLUSIONS

5. Raoul recognizes the ghost as
   (A) Christine's father (B) his brother (C) the Persian
   (D) the death's head from Perros.

USING YOUR REASON

6. Madame Giry was rehired in her job because
   (A) nobody else was as good at the job as she was
   (B) the ghost insisted she be rehired (C) Richard admired
   her honesty (D) only she could communicate directly
   with the ghost.

7. The Opera ghost went to the Masked Ball because
   (A) he wears a mask anyhow (B) Christine wanted to go
   out (C) he wanted to meet Raoul (D) he wanted to terror-
   ize the guests.

THINKING IT OVER

8. Christine accuses Raoul of losing faith in her. Why does
   she think that? Why does Raoul say the things he says?

Chapters 11-13

FINDING THE MAIN IDEA

1. Raoul and Christine make secret plans to
   (A) get married (B) run away (C) kill Erik (D) unmask the ghost.
2. Christine learns that the voice is a monster. But she does not hate him because
   (A) he writes wonderful music (B) he gives her good lessons (C) he loves her (D) he treats her like a queen.

REMEMBERING DETAILS

3. Raoul and Christine went exploring all over the Opera, except for
   (A) the gardens (B) the prop rooms (C) the roof (D) the cellars.
4. Raoul is supposed to leave on an expedition
   (A) to the North Pole (B) to the South Pole (C) around the world (D) to the Orient.
5. Erik wants his composition *Don Juan Triumphant* to be
   (A) buried with him (B) performed as an opera (C) burned when he dies (D) given as a requiem.

DRAWING CONCLUSIONS

6. When Christine went away for two days, she probably went
   (A) to Perros (B) to see Madame Valérius (C) to see the Angel. (D) none of these
7. Why will Christine not run away with Raoul?
   (A) She wants to finish her performances. (B) She wants the voice to hear her sing. (C) She believes there is no danger. (D) She wants to delay marriage.

USING YOUR REASON

8. Christine refused to recognize Raoul in her dressing room because
   (A) she could not see clearly (B) she had told the Angel she was only friends with Raoul (C) she didn't know who he was (D) she knew she could not marry him.
9. Count Philippe does not approve of the romance because
   (A) Christine is a singer (B) Christine is too young (C) Christine was married before (D) he wants to arrange a different marriage for Raoul.

IDENTIFYING THE MOOD

10. While Raoul and Christine are talking on the roof of the Opera, they hear sounds. The writer creates a feeling of (A) safety (B) nervousness (C) playfulness (D) terror.

THINKING IT OVER

11. Christine asks Raoul to promise that he will make her go away with him by force if necessary. She says, "I fear that if I go back this time, I won't ever return." What does Christine think might happen? Find some evidence from the story to support your response.

Chapters 14-17

FINDING THE MAIN IDEA

1. The two Opera managers are behaving very strangely because (A) Christine Daaé has disappeared (B) Mme. Giry will not talk to them (C) 20,000 francs have disappeared (D) they are afraid of the ghost.

REMEMBERING DETAILS

2. When Mercier finally got the managers to open their door, Moncharmin put into his hand (A) a thousand francs (B) a safety pin (C) a key to his office (D) a program.

3. Mme. Giry put the envelope on the ledge in Box 5. Then (A) she sneaked back in and took it (B) the ghost came and got it (C) nobody touched it (D) it disappeared.

4. Mme. Giry boxed Richard on the ear because (A) he locked her in an office (B) he called her an idiot (C) he grabbed the envelope (D) he called her a thief.

5. The managers needed a safety pin to (A) pin the envelope to Richard's pocket (B) pin a note to the money (C) pin Richard's pocket closed (D) unlock the desk.

DRAWING CONCLUSIONS

6. When the Persian tells Raoul "Erik's secrets concern no one but himself," he probably means (A) not to talk about Erik (B) not to tell about the lake (C) not to tell about Mme. Giry (D) not to try to trace Christine.

7. Madame Giry believes in the ghost mostly because (A) she has heard him speak (B) he declared Meg would be an empress (C) he leaves her candy (D) she is superstitious.

USING YOUR REASON
8. Raoul looked for a gate at the Rue Scribe because (A) he wanted to find the entrance to the lake (B) he knew Christine would wait there (C) he knew Erik would wait there (D) he was in a hurry.
9. Gabriel and Mercier locked Mme. Giry in an office because (A) they were told to (B) they needed to be sure of where she was every minute (C) she boxed Richard on the ear (D) they thought she was a thief.

THINKING IT OVER
10. The ghost used Madame Giry to collect the money from Moncharmin and Richard. How did the money disappear from the envelope that the managers put it in?

Chapters 18-20

FINDING THE MAIN IDEA
1. The Persian tells Raoul he will take him to Christine because (A) he works for the police (B) he is Philippe's friend (C) he feels sorry for Raoul (D) he hates Erik.

REMEMBERING DETAILS
2. When Raoul uses the name "Erik," the Persian hushes him because (A) he does not want to attract the ghost's attention (B) he does not like the name "Erik" (C) the name "Erik" means "the devil" (D) he does not want the police commissioner to hear.
3. Darius is (A) the dressing-room manager (B) the Persian's servant (C) Christine Daaé's loyal servant (D) a singer.
4. The Persian knows about secret doors and mirrors because (A) he built them (B) he found them (C) he has watched Erik come and go (D) he was once a member of the secret police.

5. The three bodies in the cellar, the gas men, are
   (A) drunk (B) drugged (C) dead (D) bound and gagged.

DRAWING CONCLUSIONS

6. When the Persian says, "I don't hate him. If I did, he would
   have been stopped a long time ago," he probably means
   (A) he loves Erik (B) he created Erik (C) he could have
   taken Erik's life once (D) he is more powerful than Erik.
7. When the Persian and Raoul see the head of fire, it turns
   out to be
   (A) the daroga (B) an optical illusion (C) Erik's servant
   (D) the rat catcher.

USING YOUR REASON

8. Commissioner Mifroid tells Raoul that his brother
   kidnapped Christine because
   (A) he wants to get Raoul out of the way (B) he wants to
   handle the investigation himself (C) he believes Philippe
   did it (D) he wants to impress the managers.
9. There are trapdoors in the Opera house so that
   (A) Erik can come and go as he pleases (B) people can live
   below the stage without being seen (C) props can be raised
   and lowered easily (D) scene-changers will not get lost.

IDENTIFYING THE MOOD

10. As the Persian and Raoul go through the mirror, the
    Persian's directions and movements create a feeling of
    (A) humor (B) dismay (C) sadness (D) mystery.
11. As the head of fire and the strange noise approach, the two
    men feel
    (A) confident (B) terrified (C) amused (D) confused.

THINKING IT OVER

12. The Persian seems to know a great deal about Erik. What
    do you think his relationship to "the monster" might be?
    Why does he fear Erik?

Chapters 21-24

FINDING THE MAIN IDEA

1. The Persian wasn't surprised at Christine's disappearance because
   (A) he had watched Erik with Christine (B) he knew Carlotta was jealous (C) he knew Raoul had made plans (D) he did not trust her.
2. Erik designed the torture chamber with the tree for
   (A) growing fruit (B) shade (C) hanging oneself (D) amusement.

REMEMBERING DETAILS.

3. The Persian had made Raoul keep his hand up in front of his face, at eye level, in order to
   (A) ward off flying objects (B) protect his eyes from the glare (C) protect against the Punjab lasso (D) provide protection from the evil eye.
4. The job of the siren is to
   (A) protect the Persian (B) protect the lake (C) protect the house (D) frighten off intruders.
5. At first, Christine cannot help the two men because
   (A) she is tied up (B) the monster is watching (C) the door is locked (D) she has fainted.
6. The torture chamber becomes
   (A) a mirage (B) a lake (C) a tropical forest.
   (D) none of these

DRAWING CONCLUSIONS

7. Erik sings a requiem for the man who rang the bell because
   (A) he wrote the music (B) he killed the man (C) he is grateful to the man (D) he hopes the man has died.
8. The Persian tells Raoul that he will find the trick of the door in one hour. But he wants Raoul to be quiet because
   (A) he needs to concentrate (B) he does not want Erik to hear them (C) he is afraid Raoul is going mad (D) he wants Raoul to preserve his strength.

USING YOUR REASON

9. The Persian decides to rescue Christine from Erik because

194

(A) he likes Raoul (B) he thinks Erik has gone too far this
time (C) he likes Christine's singing (D) he loves Christine.
10. Erik feels indebted to the Persian because
(A) he created the monster (B) he saved the monster's life
(C) he knows all about the monster (D) he taught the monster all he knows.
11. When the men discover the gunpowder, the Persian throws
the lantern far away because
(A) it would set off the powder (B) he does not want
Raoul to see the powder (C) he is very angry at being
tricked (D) he is despairing because it is not water.

THINKING IT OVER
12. Why is the Persian so much calmer than Raoul? Why is
he so sure that he can find a way out? Find some evidence
from the text to support your response.

Chapters 25-26, Epilogue

FINDING THE MAIN IDEA
1. Christine decided to stay with Erik. Which of the following was probably *not* a reason?
(A) Christine wanted to save Raoul's life. (B) Christine
did love Erik. (C) Christine wanted to save all the people
in the opera. (D) Christine wanted to learn more from
Erik's lessons.

REMEMBERING DETAILS
2. The monster chose eleven o'clock for Christine's decision
because
(A) there would be a lot of people in the Opera House
(B) Christine was scheduled to sing at that time
(C) he was born at that time (D) he needed time to
assemble the gunpowder barrels.
3. Turning the scorpion means that Christine
(A) will escape from Erik (B) will marry Erik (C) will
die with everyone (D) will never marry.
4. When the Persian wakes up, he sees that Christine appears
(A) laughing and happy (B) calm and peaceful
(C) frightened and hysterical (D) dazed and ill.

DRAWING CONCLUSIONS

5. When Erik says the grasshopper will "hop to our wedding," Christine knows
   (A) which insect to turn (B) that Erik will trick her (C) that Raoul will die (D) that Erik has gone mad.
6. Erik puts Raoul in the Communists' dungeon in order to
   (A) keep him from Christine (B) keep the house at the lake a secret (C) kill him (D) taunt him.

USING YOUR REASON

7. Which of these are part of the explanation given for the "ghost" in Box 5?
   (A) trapdoors (B) large columns (C) ventriloquism (D) all of these
8. Erik comes to talk to the Persian at the end. Which of the following reasons explain why he did that?
   (A) He wants the Persian to know what has happened to him, to Christine, and to Raoul. (B) He wants the Persian to know how much he loves Christine. (C) He wants to ask the Persian to do a favor for him. (D) all of these

THINKING IT OVER

9. In the final chapter, Erik visits the Persian. After reading Chapter 26, did your opinion of Erik change? If so, how? If it did not, why not?
10. From the Epilogue, what do you learn about where Raoul and Christine are? Why are they there?